A
HOUSE
WITHOUT
MIRRORS

Pushkin Children's Books
71-75 Shelton Street
London, WC2H 9JQ

A House without Mirrors first published in Swedish as
Ett hus utan speglar by Rabén & Sjögren in 2012

Original text © Rabén & Sjögren, 2012
Translation © Karin Altenberg 2013

This edition published by Pushkin Children's Books in 2013

ISBN 978-1-78269-007-8

Translation of this work was supported by a grant from the
Swedish Arts Council.

Set in 12 on 19 Berling Nova by Tetragon, London

Printed and bound in Italy by Printer Trento SRL
on Munken Print White 100gsm

www.pushkinpress.com

A HOUSE

WITHOUT MIRRORS

Mårten Sandén

Illustrations by Moa Schulman

Translated from the Swedish by Karin Altenberg

PUSHKIN CHILDREN'S BOOKS

"One hundred! Ready or not, here I come!"

Chapter One

HIDE-AND-SEEK

"One *hundred*! Ready or not, here I come!"

The echo of my cry bounced around the hall in Henrietta's house for a moment before dying out. As silence returned I could hear the creaking of the parquet floors upstairs. It was my cousins looking for places to hide.

We played hide-and-seek nearly every day, but I rarely got to be the seeker. Both Wilma and Erland said that it wouldn't be fair, as I could find my way around Henrietta's house so much better than they could. I suppose they were right, as Dad always let me tag along when he was looking after Henrietta, but it's still not much fun when you hardly ever get to be the seeker.

And, besides, you'd have expected my cousins to know their way around by then. Wilma and her mum, Dad's sister Kajsa, had arrived over three weeks before, and Erland and Signe had been here since school broke up. Their dad, Uncle Daniel, worked at the university, so he had the summers off.

But no one had been at Henrietta's house as long as me and Dad. Apart from Henrietta herself, of course.

The afternoon light fell through the stained-glass mosaic in the window up above the stairs and seeped out in pale-coloured stains across the floor in the hall. The floor was black and white, like a chessboard, and sometimes I remembered playing a sort of pretend chess there when I was little. I remembered the feeling very clearly, and I remembered that somebody else was there with me. Henrietta, perhaps, in the days when she could still walk on her own.

I quickly searched the ground floor. There weren't that many places to hide, as Henrietta had sold or given away most of her furniture since she'd been living here alone. Dad says that she'd been preparing for death for a long time.

Many of the rooms were completely empty now; just some junk against the walls, or a cupboard too heavy to be moved. When you're playing hide-and-seek, that emptiness is good for the seeker and bad for the hiders.

I slunk through the dining room, the parlours and lounges and the corner room, which was called the Office, and continued towards the conservatory, which was a large, glassed-in room at the back of the house.

There was no one there, and no one in the kitchen or the pantry either. Not even Signe, my youngest cousin. Signe usually hid close to the kitchen because she was a little afraid of the dark.

On the great stairs leading up to the first floor and the drawing rooms, I stopped and listened. The creaking had stopped; they had probably all found places to hide. They could be anywhere.

Dad said that he hardly knew how many rooms there were in Henrietta's house, but that was just him talking. He knew as well as I did that there were nineteen. Twenty with the conservatory. Ten of the rooms were bedrooms—if you counted the two tiny ones behind the kitchen that used to be the cook's room and the maid's room, when Henrietta and my great-grandfather were kids nearly a hundred years ago.

I had barely started looking through the drawing rooms when I saw somebody standing on the stairs leading up to the second floor. At first I thought it was Erland lurking there in the shadows on the landing with his arms hanging down beside him. But luckily it wasn't. It was Signe, Erland's little sister.

"What's up, Signe?" I asked. "Can't you find a place to hide?"

Signe shook her head. She looked frightened. Both Erland and Uncle Daniel treated Signe as if she were a dimwit, just because she never said anything. She wasn't. She just didn't like talking.

I went up to the landing where Signe was standing and reached out my hand towards her.

"Come," I said. "I'll help you."

Signe took my hand and together we climbed the stairs towards the bedrooms. When we reached the dark corridor leading to my room, I could feel Signe's hand tightening around mine. I squeezed her hand back.

She could have hidden in my room, or the one Dad sometimes slept in, but I reckoned that the one at the end of the corridor would be a bit more exciting.

It was a large octagonal room where Henrietta's English mother used to keep her clothes over a hundred years ago. It was empty now, but there were plenty of wardrobes to hide in.

"Here, sweetie," I said, pushing her into the room. "Choose whichever door you want, okay?"

Signe watched me with her solemn grey eyes while I checked there were no keys left in any of the half-opened wardrobe doors. There weren't, not even in the middle one, which was locked.

"Okay, Signe? Just hide in one of the wardrobes, whichever one you like."

She was only five, and you had to spell everything out to her. Sometimes you really couldn't be sure that she'd understood, but this time she actually nodded.

"Good," I said, and stroked her hair. "Hide now, and I'll come and find you in a little while."

I didn't wait to see which wardrobe she entered. That would have been cheating.

Carrying my shoes in my hand, I sneaked back down the stairs to the drawing rooms again. I knew exactly which steps squeaked and I avoided them carefully.

The great challenge of being a seeker was finding Wilma. She came up with hiding places you'd never think of. Once she was hiding inside the grand piano

9

in the downstairs parlour, lying on top of the strings with the lid down. Erland was the seeker, and he never found her. When Wilma told us where she had been, Erland blabbed to his dad, Uncle Daniel, and Wilma got a right telling-off.

Uncle Daniel probably thought that kids shouldn't play at all, and we were not allowed to call him just Daniel. We had to call him Uncle Daniel, although he was only just a bit older than Dad. It didn't bother me, though. He really was just like a boring old man.

The first three drawing rooms closest to the stairs were empty. The large dining room and the nursery too. I went through them rather quickly as it was usually Erland who hid there. I preferred not to find him.

"Psst."

I didn't even turn my head when I heard the hiss. No one could *psst* as creepily as Erland. Like a snake with a tiny giggle hiding under the hissing.

"Erland is tagged," I said. "On top of the wardrobe."

He was already on his way back down when I turned around. Normally Erland got angry when you beat him at something, but this time he didn't seem to mind.

"Bravo," he said, looking at me with that grin that I hated. "Aren't you the clever one?"

Erland was only seven, but he was not at all like a child. He walked slowly and talked like a little old man. Just like his dad, come to think of it. Perhaps that's not all that strange, as Erland and Signe lived alone with Uncle Daniel. No one ever mentioned their mum, but I was pretty sure she wasn't dead.

I walked towards the hall and could hear Erland sneaking after me. He followed me up towards the second floor too.

"Will you help me find Wilma, then?" I said over my shoulder, hoping he'd say no.

But Erland didn't say yes or no. With a few quick steps he overtook me and placed himself in my way at the top of the stairs.

"Look at this, Thomasine, puke-medicine," he said, pulling something that looked like false teeth out of his pocket. "Look out so I don't bite you!"

He clacked the false teeth like castanets and they grinned at me, unnervingly like a real mouth.

"Give me a break," I said. "Where did you get hold of?..."

I felt a lump in my stomach as I realized.

They were Henrietta's dentures. Erland must have crept up and taken them out of the glass on her bedside table when Dad wasn't looking.

"Are you crazy? You can't just steal her teeth!"

Erland only laughed and skulked off along the corridor—straight into Dad.

"What's going on?" Dad said.

He didn't sound angry. Not even when he saw the false teeth that Erland didn't have time to hide. Dad never sounded angry, just sad and tired.

"Was it you who took them, Erland?" he said. "Henrietta needs them. She can't eat properly without."

Erland stared down at his feet.

"Somebody else must have nicked them," he said. "I just found them."

The way in which Erland told lies made me furious. He always got that trembling, miserable tone in his voice. As if you were supposed to feel sorry for him.

"Cut it out, Erland," I snapped. "Who else would be as mean and dumb and—"

Dad held up a tired hand, and as always I shut up straight away.

"That's enough, Thomasine," he said. "Could you leave them on the stairs please, Erland? I'll take them with me when I go back up again."

Erland didn't answer, but he walked towards the attic stairs that led up to the room where Henrietta was lying.

Erland was actually the only one, except for me and Dad, who ever went up to see Henrietta. Dad did it because he had to, and I did it because I wanted to help him out, but Erland had no real reason for sneaking around up there in the attic room. I think he was hoping that Henrietta would die while he was watching.

As soon as I was alone I sank down on the top step and let my hair fall over my face. I felt completely empty inside, but I knew I wouldn't cry. Not this time.

At times, nearly every day, there were moments when I didn't know how I would make it through the summer, or even the next hour. I didn't belong in this silent house. The people who claimed to be my family felt like strangers.

I hardly recognized Dad any more.

"Hello? Thomasine? Is anyone seeking, or what?"

Wilma stood on the landing between the first and second floor, and I calmed down when I saw her, as I always did. If it wasn't for Wilma I'm not sure I'd have had the energy to stay on.

I got up and wiped the hair out of my eyes.

"No, let's stop," I said, starting to walk down the stairs towards her. "I can't be bothered any more."

"Fine," said Wilma. "Anyway, Mum's here with the pizzas."

When I reached her she put her arm around me.

Wilma was still a bit taller than me, even though I was catching up, and her arm felt good around my shoulders. Kind and warm, almost like Mum's.

"Erland is mental," I said. "Can you believe that he'd taken Henrietta's false teeth? He was playing with them!"

Wilma stopped and looked at me.

"Henrietta has false teeth?" she whispered. "Seriously?"

At first I couldn't tell if she was joking, but then I saw that she wasn't. Quite often it feels as if Wilma is the younger of the two of us.

"Wilma, she is over a hundred years old," I said. "Of course she has false teeth."

"I met someone," she said, taking my hand.
"We played for a while."

Chapter Two

THE GIRL WHO DISAPPEARED

W e didn't say anything else as we walked down the stairs to the ground floor, passing through the parlours, lounges, the dining room and into the pantry. I smelt the pizza even before I heard the voices from the kitchen. Up until then I had been quite hungry, but as usual it didn't last. Before we came to Henrietta's house I sometimes craved pizza. I didn't think I'd ever crave pizza again. When it was their turn to make dinner, both Kajsa and Daniel bought pizza one, if not two, evenings each week. Sometimes we ended up having pizza four times a week.

Erland, who was already sitting at the table, must have come down the back stairs from the second floor. Uncle Daniel was sitting next to him, reading a paper, and Kajsa was standing up, unpacking the pizzas from a paper bag. Kajsa was still wearing her coat, and even from a distance you could see how grumpy she was.

"Typical, they're ice-cold again," she snarled, poking in one of the pizza cartons. "It's so bloody annoying never getting home while they're still warm! Surely there's a pizzeria somewhere closer?"

Uncle Daniel looked up and scratched the stubble on his chin.

"Never mind," he said. "We can eat them cold, can't we?"

While Wilma and I sat down, Kajsa walked over to the ancient Husqvarna stove.

"You can sit there and eat cold pizza if you like," she said, turning on the oven. "But I'm not going to."

Dad came down the back stairs and went straight to the cupboard to measure out Henrietta's medicine. He hardly lifted his head while he moved through the room. It was as if we weren't there.

Kajsa and Dad had the same colour eyes, and before Dad grew a beard there was a certain similarity between him and Uncle Daniel too. But now they were no more alike than strangers sitting beside each other on the bus. You'd never have guessed that they were brothers and sister.

Suddenly Dad looked up.

"Where is Signe?"

Signe. A cold wave of shame and anxiety started at my scalp and ran down my back. No one had told Signe that our game of hide-and-seek was over. Fear prickling my skin, I stood up and walked towards the door.

"I'll let her know."

Climbing the stairs, I tried to calm down in the way I always do. It was going to be all right. Wilma and I had only been back down in the kitchen for a couple of minutes. There was nothing dangerous on the second floor, and Signe was not lost. As far as she knew, we were still playing the game. There hadn't even been time for her to get scared.

I told myself all that, but it didn't help. The old fear never went away; it just lurked beneath the surface, and anything could arouse it. As soon as I reached the corridor I started calling her.

"Signe? Signe, sweetie, you can come out now!"

No answer, and as I stopped in the doorway I could see that the room where I had left her was empty.

"Signe? Supper is ready."

The octagonal room with its narrow wardrobe doors was silent. There was nothing that scared me as much as that heavy, empty silence. I looked behind the boxes and rubbish bags, although I knew no one could be hiding there. Not even skinny little Signe.

"You can come out now, Signe. You've won!"

I tried to sound cheerful, but that only made things worse. The silence could tell that I was lying, and it twisted my voice into something horrible and evil. My fingers sweaty, I started prying open the wardrobe doors, one after the other. I called Signe's name into the darkness, and each time silence shouted back at me.

Finally, the only door remaining was the locked one in the middle. Could she have got in there? No, I had checked, hadn't I? That wardrobe had been locked and there had been no key in the lock. I knocked anyway.

"Signe?" I whispered through the keyhole. "Please, Signe, come out. You're the winner!"

A cool breath of wind seeped out of the keyhole and brushed my lips. It felt like a kiss.

I carried on calling her while I searched all the bedrooms on the second floor, as well as my own room and the one used by Dad. Fear had taken hold of me for so long now that I began to feel numb. Dad says you can't carry on being really afraid for more than a short period at a time, and he's right.

"I'll have to get Wilma," I muttered while I walked towards the stairs. "I'll fetch Wilma, and then we'll search—"

"I'm here, Thomasine."

The voice behind me brought to mind the angel chimes that Mum used to light on the dinner table at Christmas. I could almost see the little ornament before me: the flames that pushed the wheel with the angels around and around and the silver bells that chimed lightly and delicately.

But as I turned around it was not an angel standing there. It was Signe.

"Signe, where have you been?"

Signe smiled at me as I reached out my hand to her. She seemed completely unharmed.

"I met someone," she said, taking my hand. "We played for a while."

I didn't understand what she meant, but I was mainly thinking how strange it was to hear her voice. Of course I'd heard Signe speak before,

but not that often, and hardly ever in complete sentences.

"Okay," I said. "Great. Shall we go and eat?"

I thought to myself that my voice sounded hoarse and frightened, but Signe didn't seem to notice. She simply held her little hand around my finger and skipped down the stairs. She was just the same as ever, or even a bit cheerful in fact, and I started feeling better.

Nothing had happened. Signe was unharmed and seemed to have enjoyed playing hide-and-seek. I had not been looking after her, but this time everything had been fine.

Wilma glanced at me.

Chapter Three

SIGNE SPEAKS

Kajsa was kneeling by the oven door. She was still wearing her coat and wellies, her blonde hair gathered back in a hard, taut ponytail.

"Who ordered a calzone?"

No one replied. No one ever ordered calzone, but Kajsa always bought one in any case, every time.

"Ah well," she said grumpily. "I suppose I'll have to eat it myself then."

She always said that too, every time.

"Is there one with pineapple on it?"

Everyone froze, as if they didn't understand where the clear, tiny voice was coming from.

Only Dad and I looked at Signe.

"What was that, Signe?" Dad said carefully, as if he didn't want to frighten her. "Would you like one with pineapple? A Hawaii?"

Signe nodded.

"I like Hawaii," she said loud and clear. "I like pineapple."

Kajsa gave a short laugh, but you could tell she was still grumpy.

"Holy Moses, the child speaks!" she said. "Well, well, I suppose she can have some of Thomas's, then."

Dad nodded and Signe smiled, showing all her teeth. I don't think I'd ever seen her do that before.

"Thomas can have some of my pizza," she said. "We can swap so that it's all fair."

She really was completely different. It was strange, but at the same time it felt quite normal. As if something inside Signe had suddenly been turned on.

The mood around the table brightened after she had said that thing about the pizza. Not happier, exactly, but more animated. Uncle Daniel, particularly, looked at Signe more often than he normally would, and he even stroked her cheek once. I was thinking how weird it was that everyone was so surprised, because we all knew that Signe could speak. It was just that she wouldn't normally do so.

The rare good spirits lasted for at least ten minutes, with no one quarrelling with anyone else. But at about the same time that Erland slid off his chair and sneaked out without saying thank you, the conversation slipped back into the same old pattern as always.

"So what's new, Thomas?" Kajsa said, wiping her mouth roughly with a napkin.

Dad, who was huddled over his pizza with that distant look in his eyes, looked up.

"What?"

"How's she doing?" Kajsa said again. "Any change?"

Dad looked around as if he couldn't really be sure who we all were. It occurred to me that he had gone somewhere far inside himself.

"What?" he said again. "Sorry, I was just..."

His voice died out in an apologetic mumble.

"Has the old bag said anything?" Kajsa said slowly and deliberately, as if she was talking to a child. "You are up there twenty hours a day, Thomas. You must have something to tell us."

But Dad just shook his head.

"She is weak," he muttered, taking another bite of his cold pizza. "It's hard to know what she wants. Sometimes you can tell that she wants some water, or—"

"She wants water?" Kajsa was almost yelling. "Well, isn't that great? It's bloody perfect!"

As she stood up the legs of the chair screeched against the stone floor. She threw her napkin onto her half-eaten pizza and started folding the pizza cartons with angry, jerky movements.

"But, Kajsa—"

"This won't do, Thomas!" Kajsa interrupted, staring at Dad. "Can't you see that I have a business to run? Kjell's struggling to keep up with the books, and Wilma's missed almost a month's worth of riding lessons!"

Dad opened his hands in a helpless gesture. Then he pushed the last bit of pizza into his mouth, and after chewing for a little while his eyes disappeared into the distance again.

"Go home, then," said Daniel with an annoying little smile. "No one's forcing you to stay, are they?"

Kajsa turned to him. Her eyes looked as if she were peering at a snake.

"That would suit you just fine, Daniel, wouldn't it?"

Her voice was quieter now, but just as angry.

Wilma glanced at me and I saw that her throat

and cheeks were flushed. I knew exactly what she was thinking. Nearly every night we had discussed how hard it was when the grown-ups fought. Dad never fought, of course. But that was almost as bad.

"I have to ring Kjell," Kajsa muttered, taking her squashed-up pizza carton to the sink. "Not that I have a clue what to say to him."

Wilma rolled her eyes and sort of glanced towards the place in the ceiling where her room was. I nodded carefully, so that only Wilma could see.

She got down from the table first, then Uncle Daniel and Signe. Dad and I stayed in the kitchen to clear up.

There was no washing-up to do, exactly, but I flattened the pizza cartons and placed them on top of the others on the pile by the stove. Dad was rinsing the glasses with his shoulders hunched up; his entire back was tense and stiff.

"Thanks for supper," I said when I was ready. "I'll go up and see Wilma for a while before I go to bed."

Dad turned his head. At first it was as if he couldn't see me, or didn't know who I was. Then there was a little smile, like a brief glimpse of sunshine through a cloud.

"Sleep well, sweetheart," he said, and grew serious again. "Don't forget to call Mum."

Sometimes I remembered what Dad's eyes looked like before Martin died. They were completely different. Rounder, and sort of glossier, and I wondered if they weren't bluer too. How could eyes change that much?

"Blame my mum."

Chapter Four

In Wilma's Room

"Ah, it's driving me mad! Why does it have to fall over all the time?"

I got up from Wilma's bed and walked over to the desk where she was sitting.

The little pocket mirror she'd borrowed from Kajsa had slid down once again until it lay flat on the tabletop. I picked it up, then fetched a book from the pile on the floor and propped it in front of the mirror as a support.

"Thanks, Tommy," Wilma sighed, pulling the top off her eyeliner pen. "Remind me again, why don't they have any proper mirrors here?"

That was the strange thing about Wilma's voice. It changed according to whom she was speaking to.

When she was with her mum she spoke quietly and rarely, and with her so-called friends from school she sounded stupid and giggly. But when it was just the two of us, her voice sounded the way it was supposed to be. I loved Wilma's real voice. She was the only person in the whole world who called me Tommy.

"Henrietta had them removed," I said, picking up another book and flicking through it. "When she left the theatre."

The book was in English, a novel about vampires. It wasn't really my kind of thing, but Wilma liked that sort of stuff. She read really thick books set in fantasy worlds, about knights and wizards. I put the book back on the pile and saw Wilma's eyes squint into the tiny mirror as she drew a black line across her eyelid. Her eyes always looked strange and small when they weren't being enlarged by the thick lenses of her glasses.

"Did she think that she had grown ugly?" she said. "Or, you know, old?"

"I don't know," I said, and it was true. "I don't think she was all that bothered about that sort of thing. Dad said that she wasn't at all vain back when she used to appear in the newspapers."

"Me neither," said Wilma quickly. "Vain, I mean."

I didn't know what to say. Wilma was sensitive about her appearance, especially when she was about to meet up with the girls from her class. They were always talking about clothes and hairstyles and that kind of stuff.

Wilma went to school in another part of the city, some distance away. I'd only been there once, to see a school cabaret that Wilma had written the script for, but that was enough for me never to want to go again. I was freezing the whole evening, although the hall wasn't particularly cold. The chill came from the way Wilma's schoolmates and their parents looked at Dad and me. Or, rather, how they avoided looking at us. No one even asked who I was, and they talked to each other in a way that made you feel stupid. Mum said it was a school for snobs and it was a shame that Wilma had to go there.

According to Wilma it was a good school, and you could get into any college if you got good grades from there. It might be true, I don't know.

"When is the party?" I asked. "Not tonight, is it?"

"Tomorrow," Wilma said. "I'm just trying out some new make-up. Actually, I don't really want to go."

In spite of the fact that only people in her class were going to the party, and in spite of the fact that she always says that she couldn't care less about them, Wilma had bought one hundred and fifty kronor worth of make-up. A new dress too, and Kajsa had helped her pick it. I wondered if I would be like that too when I reached ninth grade. It was only two years away. Would I suddenly find myself spending a whole hour sitting like that, trying out my make-up, just because I was going to a party the next day? It seemed unlikely.

Wilma moved the eyeliner to her left eye and I held my breath. It was her right eye that was the weak one. I knew she could hardly see a thing when she closed her left eye.

"But you have to make a bit of an effort," Wilma said, drawing a shaky line across her fair eyelashes. "Life gets easier if you look nice."

This time it was Kajsa's voice I heard, sort of breathing under Wilma's own.

Kajsa had probably once used exactly those words, and they had lodged themselves in Wilma like the truth. She paused with her eyeliner in the air and turned to me.

"You are lucky, you are, Tommy," she said. "Your eyes were already made up when you were born."

Before I could help myself, my hand flew up to the point where my black eyebrows almost met just above my nose.

"Blame my mum," I mumbled. "If she hadn't plucked her eyebrows they would have looked just like mine."

Wilma replaced the top of her eyeliner and opened a tube of mascara.

"I know, we read about it at school," she said. "If one parent has dark hair and brown eyes the kids get them as well. It's a law of nature, like."

"But not always," I said. "The dark one can have a light predisposition, and then the child can end up blonde anyway. That's the way it was with..."

I fell silent, but it was too late. Wilma looked at me with her partly made-up eyes.

"That's how it was with your little brother," she said slowly. "You think of Martin nearly all the time, don't you?"

I looked down at my shoes and shrugged.

"Mum says..." I tried, but it wasn't as easy as that, of course. My voice thickened and I had to wait a few seconds before I could carry on.

"Mum says you have to move on. Hold on to the memories and let go of the grief."

"That's the most stupid thing I've ever heard!" said Wilma. "As if you could just make up your mind about it!"

When we were alone Wilma came right out with things like that, even if she'd never dare to say them if somebody else was there. But it felt good when she did. The air immediately grew cooler, and it became easier to breathe.

"Kajsa hates it when anyone cries," Wilma said as she started to colour her eyelashes with small, firm strokes of the brush. "It must run in the family."

"But my mum doesn't belong to this family," I said.

Wilma looked up, really surprised.

"She doesn't?"

"No," I said, shaking my head. "Mum's not related to anyone here apart from me."

Wilma was quiet for a moment. Then she sighed.

"No, that's right," she said. "It's Thomas and my mum who are related to Henrietta. Jesus, I can never keep all that stuff in my head. She is sort of their aunt, isn't she?"

"Great-aunt," I said. "Henrietta was the younger sister of *my* great-grandfather on my dad's side, who was *your* great-grandfather on your mum's side, and—"

"Okay, okay, okay!" Wilma said, waving a pink lipstick wildly in the air. "So she's the great-aunt-granny-aunt to my great-grandmother's second cousin's cousin. That's what I said all along!"

I laughed. "Okay."

"That's it," Wilma said, throwing away the tissue that she'd wiped her lipstick on. "Does this look all right for tomorrow?"

"Lovely," I said. "You look a lot older, kind of."

Wilma turned her head and looked at her reflection in her pocket mirror. She didn't seem to like what she saw.

"But do I look cuter?"

I shouldn't have hesitated, of course, but I did. For maybe only a fraction of a second, but it was enough.

"Sure, absolutely. But you also look lovely just the way you are."

Wilma looked serious, almost impassive. But without warning a tear welled out of her right eye, the weak one.

"Thanks," she said in a completely normal voice with the tear rolling down her cheek, leaving a grey snail trail of make-up in its wake. "But you don't have to lie, Tommy. I know that I'm fat and ugly."

"But you are not ugly! You are..."

I went completely cold when her round face screwed up in tears, like a clown's mask. Wilma's weeping could be so forceful that it scared me. Like watching an accident happen. Her shoulders started shaking, but there was no sound. I wanted to soothe her, say something that would help, but there was nothing I could say.

"Why?" she sobbed. "Why didn't I turn out pretty? Like Mum."

My own eyes grew dim and my nose pricked. I still didn't know what to say, but I leant forward and held Wilma while she cried. Her large, warm body shook in my skinny arms and I pushed my mouth into the soft curls at her ear.

"I don't know, Wilma," I whispered. "I don't know."

If only they knew.

Chapter Five

A PRAYER

I only started to cry when I was by myself again. That's how it always happened.

I lay there in my bed in Henrietta's house, and felt wave upon wave of weeping washing through me. The waves began like a tickling in the stomach, and they continued in a rolling cramp that pressed the air out of my lungs and up through my throat. There was nothing I could do to hold back the tears, but I could at least stay quiet. I was always able to do that.

I think I inherited my silent crying from Dad. On quite a few occasions I walked into Henrietta's room and saw him sitting with his face buried in the duvet and her hand in his. There was no sound, but you could tell from his back that he was crying. I always went before he saw me.

When the tears finally dried up I was no longer

sleepy. The house was quiet all around me, so the others had probably gone to bed. I wrapped the duvet like a mantle round my shoulders, got up and walked to the window.

It was a clear night, with a full moon and lots of stars in the sky. A man with a dog was passing by, and he stopped by the garden gate. Both the dog and the man lifted their heads towards the house with the dark windows. I often saw people doing that, and every time I wondered what they saw. How much did they really know about those of us who lived in Henrietta's house?

Some things were known to everyone in the neighbourhood, of course. The house had been here for over a century, and our family had owned it all this time. Dad said that we used to be rich, when Granddad was little. And almost everyone knew who Henrietta was. Or at least that she used to be a famous actress and that she would soon be dead. People who regularly walked past the house probably knew that her family was here to look after her, and that we came and went, taking turns to look after her. A large, wealthy family where everyone takes care of everyone else and no one has to be alone.

If only they knew.

Uncle Daniel still had some kind of a job at the university, but Mum said that was just because they couldn't get rid of him. Erland was seriously wrong in the head, and Signe seemed afraid of almost everything. Kajsa and her husband Kjell were always busy with their advertising agency. They'd go shopping, and take Wilma out, but it was as if they were never really part of what was going on around them. Wilma said that Kjell drank wine every day, and that Kajsa probably did too but she was better at hiding it. And Wilma ate too much and Kajsa hardly anything at all.

Not that Dad and I were much better. We had been here for months now, and with every day that passed it was as if things were slipping a bit further away from us.

The world out there, and Mum too. Although she had been drifting away for a long time now, ever since Martin died.

I don't know how we ended up like this. We were a normal family once, but without anyone noticing we started falling apart. Like when the nuts are shaken loose on a bike.

When I was little, Mum, Dad and I used to do everything together. There was a kitchen table where I used to sit with my crayons and paper and do drawings for Mum. Dad used to sit opposite, writing. Once, in the library, I found books that he had written. There were several of them listed in the catalogue and I had never even heard him mention them before.

I didn't dare take Dad's books out of the library, so over the course of several weeks I went there every afternoon to read them. They were good, actually. No wizards, no murders; just stories about ordinary people living their everyday lives. The kind of stuff that I thought I would write about myself, if I could.

Dad no longer wrote. He only looked after Henrietta and me. Mum didn't want to be looked after, so he rarely saw her. They weren't divorced or anything like that, but Mum lived in our flat and Dad and I lived at Henrietta's. It felt as if it had been carrying on like this for a very long time.

Would it have been better if I had moved in with Mum?

The very thought made me panic. I couldn't leave Dad, although I didn't actually think that he needed me. And what could I do for him, anyway? I couldn't save him. Not alone.

Please help us, I thought, closing my eyes. *Make us into something different than we are. Something better.*

When I looked up again the man with the dog had vanished. It was cold by the window, so I lay back down on the bed again. My body felt empty and calm and I knew that there'd be no more crying that night.

I looked up at the ceiling and wondered why it was that Mum never cried and I cried so seldom. Why Dad only cried when he thought no one was watching.

I sometimes wondered why the whole world wasn't crying all the time.

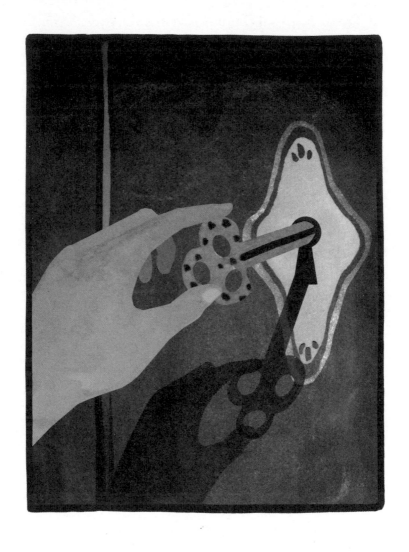

"Open the door, Thomasine!"

Chapter Six

A Nocturnal Outing

"Thomasine?"

I opened my eyes. The bedroom was white with moonlight, but it was empty. I had been dreaming about Wilma, that she was buried under snow and was calling to me. Was it her voice in the dream that had woken me up?

"Thomasine, are you asleep?"

No, I was awake. The whisper came from a tiny little form among the shadows by the door. A ghost?

"Signe?" I whispered back. "Is that you?"

The outline of the little figure took a step forward and trod straight into a moonbeam. The face was almost as pale as her white nightgown, and if it hadn't been for the smile Signe could easily have been a ghost.

"Come on," she said, reaching her hand out to me. "Come on, I want to show you something."

I turned my head and saw that the radio alarm showed 03.48.

"It's the middle of the night, Signe," I whispered. "Can't it wait until—"

"It's a secret," Signe interrupted. "You mustn't tell Erland. Nor Dad either."

She still sounded weird, just like she had at dinner. Like a completely different child. This Signe didn't seem in the slightest bit afraid. When I reached out my hand to stroke her face, she grabbed hold of my index finger.

"Come on, get up!" she said again, pulling me from the bed. "I'll show you where I was hiding."

I sighed and placed my feet on the floor.

Signe was still holding on to my finger as we tiptoed down the corridor outside my room. Henrietta's house was even quieter at night than during the day, and the thick carpet under our feet absorbed every sound. You probably could have stomped up and down without anyone hearing.

"Have you been to sleep at all, Signe?" I yawned. "Sometimes it helps if you read a book."

Signe looked up at me, surprised, and giggled.

"But I can't read, can I!"

That was true, of course. I felt dense and stupid, and I couldn't work out where we were going. It wasn't until Signe stopped in the octagonal room where I'd found her after the game of hide-and-seek that I began to wake up. The room looked the same as it had that afternoon. The same empty floor and piles of cardboard boxes and bags of clothes, the same wardrobe doors.

"So you were in here after all," I said. "Were you hiding behind the boxes?"

Signe giggled again and shook her head.

"In the wardrobe," she said. "The one with all the mirrors."

I blinked until I could see her quite clearly.

"What do you mean, mirrors?" I said. "You know there are no mirrors in this house."

"No, 'cause they're all in the wardrobe," she said, pointing towards the middle door. "Someone has put them all in there."

It didn't sound like the kind of thing you'd make up. At least not the kind of thing a five-year-old would make up. I walked across the cold floorboards, and suddenly I saw it: in the wardrobe door, which had been locked, there was now a key.

"Did you take the key, Signe?" I said, trying to sound stern. "You mustn't do that. It's dangerous, you may get yourself locked in and—"

"I didn't take it!" Signe said. "She gave it to me, she did!"

Her little face looked angry and something in her eyes told me that she was telling the truth. Perhaps Kajsa or Wilma had really given her the key to play with. I stroked her tousled hair.

"All right, but you must never lock it from the inside," I said with a yawn. "Can we go back to bed now? I'll tuck you in, if you like."

Signe's face turned smooth and childlike again. She looked disappointed.

"But you have to go inside!" she said. "You can't see anything out here, can you?"

I sighed and looked at my empty wrist. My watch was back on the bedside table.

"Just a quick look, then."

Signe beamed and tiptoed up to the door. She didn't touch the key, but watched in anticipation as I turned it in the lock.

"Open it," she whispered eagerly. "Open the door, Thomasine!"

I pulled open the wardrobe door, and the first thing I saw was that somebody was in there. The skin on my back instantly grew prickly with fear.

A moment later I realized who the stranger in the wardrobe was.

It was myself. Or rather, an image of myself, lit by moonlight from the window and reflected in the dark glass of a mirror.

"Shit," I giggled. "Shit, that scared me!"

Signe looked perplexed.

"Why were you scared?" she said, taking my hand. "There's nothing to be afraid of here, Thomasine."

She stepped over the threshold, and pulled me with her. With my legs still shaking, I let myself be led.

Moonlight filtered through the half-open door, and when my eyes had grown used to it I discovered that the wardrobe was larger than I had thought, almost like a little room. Mirrors glinted everywhere; uneven, fragmented glass surfaces in stacks against the walls.

"Wilma should see this," I said. "Is there a light switch somewhere?"

Signe shook her head.

"Okay, we can check it out tomorrow," I said. "This was really cool, Signe, but we have to go back to bed now if we…"

Even in the gloom I could tell that Signe's face was growing cross again.

"You don't get it!" she said. "You have to keep the door closed and stand still. Or it won't happen!"

I sighed.

"Okay, okay, close the door, then," I said. "But only for a bit."

I was fully awake now, and I didn't mind standing in the wardrobe with Signe for a while. I was actually rather proud that it was me that she had chosen to share her imaginary game with. The very first day when Uncle Daniel and the kids turned up at the house I had realized that Signe was similar to me. When I was her age, before Martin was born, I had lived in a world of my own. I didn't have anyone to play with either, and just like Signe I had invented my own games. Slow, dreamlike afternoons when the floor turned into an ocean of imaginary water for me to swim through, or where the clouds passing by outside the windows were magnificent cities with towers and walls.

I felt a tug inside when I thought how lonely I had been. But I hadn't really understood that back then. Something had been missing, but I didn't know what it was. Then, when I was six, Martin turned up and everything was supposed to get better. But then he disappeared, and I was all alone again.

"It's happening!"

Signe's whisper made me blink. My eyes had got used to the dark in the wardrobe and I could see the mirrors clearly now. There were at least thirty of them. There were free-standing mirrors, wall mirrors, simple bathroom mirrors and mirrors in gilt frames; big ones and small ones, round ones and square. It probably wasn't possible to find a use for them all, but Wilma would at least get her make-up mirror. I would tell her after breakfast.

"What?" I yawned. "What is supposed to happen?"

Signe pulled at my finger so that I turned towards the door.

"It's already happened," she said. "We can go out there now."

"Good."

I pushed open the wardrobe door with my free hand and let Signe pull me out into the room. The night outside the window had grown lighter, but not enough for me to make out the colours of the carpet and the furniture in the octagonal room. The light looked more like an overcast afternoon than dawn. How long had we actually been in there?

"Hello?" Signe called, quite loudly. "Little girl?"

I panicked and put my hand over her mouth.

"Quiet!" I hissed. "Have you gone mad? Daniel's bedroom is right below us!"

Signe looked up at me. Her eyes were completely calm when she removed my hand. Maybe just a little surprised.

"Dad is not here," she said. "He's back on the other side."

A shiver ran down my spine. My lungs stopped breathing and I felt as if I were falling. Signe's calm voice alone had probably been enough to scare me stiff, but now there was something else.

At once I realized that the octagonal room, which had been messy and empty when we came in, was now tidy. It also contained furniture. A strange sofa that only had a back at one end, two long rails of clothes, a white table with a mirror in a gilded iron frame, and rows of perfume bottles and glass jars.

"What have you done, Signe?" I said, my voice small and pathetic. "Where are we?"

Signe looked at me again, baffled, and in the weak light from the windows her face looked ghostlike.

"You can ask her," she said, nodding towards the door to the corridor. "She lives here."

I couldn't answer. All I could do was stare at the little girl in a sailor dress who was standing in the doorway.

"I had such a weird dream."

Chapter Seven

MEMENTO OF A DREAM

"Thomasine?"

As soon as I opened my eyes I knew I had a secret. It possessed my entire body, like a fever, or maybe happiness. I had dreamt a wonderful dream. Was I even awake?

"Thomasine, sweetheart?"

Dad was standing in the doorway, his face grey in the dawn light coming through the window.

"I had such a weird dream."

Dad rested his hand on the old-fashioned switch by the door. "Let's put the light on," he said. "So you can wake up."

I sat up so that I could lean my back against the wall and pulled the duvet up to my chin.

"I'm awake. Just let me get used to the light."

Dad looked as if he was about to say something,

but after a couple of seconds he just nodded silently and turned around.

"Dad?"

He stopped, and turned towards me again.

"Dad, what's the name of that room at the end of the corridor?"

One of those rare smiles flashed across his face then disappeared, as quickly as a flat stone skims across a surface of water.

"Are you sure you've woken up?" he said. "What room?"

"The octagonal one where Henrietta's mum kept her clothes," I said. "You told me once that she had a special name for it in English."

Dad's face showed concern, as if I'd asked him something really difficult.

"You mean Granny Adelaide," he said. "She was my dad's grandmother, so I never met her."

I wrapped the duvet closer around my drawn-up knees.

"Yes, I know that," I said. "But what did she call the room?"

Dad thought. It was a long while before he answered.

"The changing room?" he said at last. "She used to change her clothes in there, for dinner and when she was going for a walk, that sort of thing. Was that what you were thinking of?"

"Yes."

Dad looked at me, his brow still furrowed. That was how he often looked of late. As if no answer, not even the right one, was enough. He didn't say anything else, and after a while he disappeared up to Henrietta's room.

The changing room. Such silly dreams.

I lay on my back again and knew straight away that I would not go back to sleep.

The dream had started playing like a film inside my head, but I was fully awake.

Signe had woken me up—or, I had dreamt that she had—and together we had walked up to Granny Adelaide's dressing room. The changing room. It must have been the name that started it all. I saw it all clearly before me, almost as if it had happened. Signe, who walked beside me through the darkness. The wardrobe that was full of mirrors, the door we closed behind us, the room that had changed when we opened the door again.

A little girl had been standing there. A strange girl in a sailor dress.

I rolled over on my stomach and pressed my head into the pillow. My heart had started beating again. The images of the dream behind my eyelids felt real, as if I could reach out and touch them. How could they be so real?

Signe had called the girl Hetty, and together they had run on ahead.

They seemed to have met before.

I had followed them through the house from room to room decorated with furniture and pictures I'd never seen. It was Henrietta's house, but at the same time it wasn't. A bit like something familiar that becomes something strange when you look at it in a mirror.

I turned onto my back again, inhaled deeply, and breathed out. It had only been a dream, but I would tell Signe about it. She would find it amusing and perhaps we could...

What was that?

Something glinted at the corner of my eye, and I turned my head.

A mirror.

In the middle of the bedroom floor sat a little mirror in a gold frame. The glass itself was oval and framed in squiggles of cast iron painted gold, and it looked completely real.

At the same time I knew it couldn't be. It was the same mirror that had been sitting on the dressing table in my dream. Cautiously, I stretched my leg out from under my duvet and let my big toe touch the frame.

The metal was cold and hard.

Real.

"Do you still like it?"

Signe was standing in the doorway that Dad had left open. She was fully dressed, and someone had plaited her hair. Wilma, probably.

"What do you mean, do I like it?" I said. "Where does it come from?"

Signe rolled her eyes.

"From the wardrobe, of course," she said. "You took it yourself. You said you were going to give it to Wilma."

I was quiet. Two worlds had collided inside me, and I was no longer sure what was possible and what was impossible. Being inside the wardrobe had not been a dream; the mirror was proof. I now remembered how I had carried it back to my room. It had been heavy and I could feel the cast-iron frame cold against my chest through my nightgown.

"Signe, what happened last night?" I said quietly. "It feels as if we were somewhere else. Was there another house?"

Signe looked at me without answering.

"And that girl?" I said quietly. "The one you called Hetty? Was she real?"

Signe didn't answer, but her eyes turned light and dreamy. I had reminded her of something she liked to think about, even if she didn't want to talk about it.

"Hurry up and give the mirror to Wilma," she said in the end. "If Erland sees it he'll blab to everyone. Then it'll no longer be a secret."

I sank down onto the pillow again.

"Yes," I said, pressing my hands against my eyes. "I will."

Wilma's eyes met mine in the mirror.

Chapter Eight

A Mirror for Wilma

"Look, with this side you look completely normal. And with this side you look bigger!"

Wilma turned the oval mirror back and forth, back and forth.

It was just like she said: on one side there was a normal mirror, and on the other side the glass was polished so that your reflection was enlarged.

"It's a shaving mirror," I said. "I googled it and found an image of one that was almost the same."

"But where does it come from?" Wilma said, looking at her enlarged face, then turning the mirror and going back to normal again. "Whose is it?"

I got up from her unmade bed and walked to the window.

"Yours, now," I said. "But don't show it to anyone."

Wilma's room looked out over the conservatory. I gazed through the glass roof at the dried-out lily pond and benches empty of flowers. Someone was sitting on the stone floor down there. The head was bent, and the hair was covered with a woolly hat. Could it be the girl, Hetty, whom Signe had?...

No. When the figure stood up and went to the pond I saw straight away who it was. Erland was the only one to move in that sneaking, hunched-up way. I stepped back from the window.

"Did Signe show you where to find this?"

I turned around, and Wilma's eyes met mine in the mirror.

"Erland told me that Signe had found a room full of mirrors up on the second floor," she said when I didn't reply. "I thought he was lying as usual."

Could Signe really have told Erland about the mirrors? Hardly. It was more likely that he had spied on her and found out about the wardrobe that way.

"You shouldn't believe everything Erland says," I said so I didn't have to lie. "He makes a lot of stuff up."

And that was undeniably true.

Far below on the ground floor the front door closed. You noticed it more as a change in the atmosphere than as a sound, but I realized that it had to be Uncle Daniel returning with the pizzas for supper.

"Shall we go down?" I said, walking towards the door. "Dinner's ready."

I didn't make it past Wilma's desk before she grabbed my arm and held me back.

"Tommy, tell me, please," she said. "I want to know too!"

"Know what? Let go of me!"

But Wilma held my wrist tight and I knew I had to meet her gaze.

"What happened to Signe yesterday?" she said and looked straight into me. "Erland said that she had... I don't know, that something had happened to her."

I shrugged.

"Yeah, but that's Erland."

"But I saw it for myself!" Wilma said, holding on to my arm. "She turned into a completely different child in the matter of half an hour."

"She did?"

I could hear how daft I sounded, and Wilma just kept on staring at me.

"Did Signe see something, Thomasine?" she said. "Did she go inside that wardrobe?"

For a moment I considered telling her about the dream that hadn't been a dream. But the thought alone felt like I was betraying something. Or someone.

"Don't tell anyone about the mirror, okay? Not even Kajsa," I said, wriggling free. "Come on now, I'm hungry."

Uncle Daniel had bought dessert. A whole ice-cream cake from the freezer at the co-op. That had never happened before.

"Do we have something to celebrate?" Kasja said after Dad removed the pizza boxes and Uncle Daniel plonked the ice-cream cake onto the dinner table.

"Perhaps," he said, putting down a stack of plates in front of her. "I saw an estate agent today. A neighbour of someone in my department."

Kajsa leant back in her chair and crossed her arms.

"An estate agent?" she said. "Why?"

Uncle Daniel sat down next to her. That was another thing he'd never done before.

70

"To get a proper valuation," he said, almost whispering. "You can't really put a price on great big houses like this without an expert opinion."

Kajsa didn't reply, but I couldn't help myself.

"Did you see an estate agent to ask how much you would get for Henrietta's house if you sell it?" I said. "But it's not yours, is it?"

Uncle Daniel blushed and reached for the bread knife.

"Where I come from a child doesn't take part in adult conversations," he said, hard-faced. "Especially when they run the risk of going without dessert."

I felt myself reddening.

"I'm not a child," I mumbled.

Kajsa waved me aside.

"So, what did they say?" she asked. "Were they able to give you a price?"

Uncle Daniel left her waiting. First he cut a big chunk of the melting cake and let it balance on the knife above his plate. Then he cut another piece, slightly smaller, and placed it on Erland's plate.

"They have to see the house first, of course," he said finally. "But Ove—the estate agent, that is—said that it's common for a property as large as this to be sold to a property developer. For offices, or to convert it into flats."

"But what does that mean?" Kajsa said. "What does it mean in terms of money?"

Uncle Daniel pushed the knife and the plate with the cake towards Signe, glanced towards the door where Dad had disappeared, and turned to Kajsa again.

"Twenty million kronor," he said, and now he was whispering for real. "Perhaps even twenty-five with the right buyer!"

Kajsa's face didn't move, but her fingers started drumming against her arm.

"Hmm," she said. "Minus the mortgage, of course, and..."

"What mortgage?" Uncle Daniel laughed hoarsely. "There is no mortgage. Not a penny!"

He spread his hands and smiled more broadly than I had ever seen him smile before.

And yet he did not look happy.

Signe was having trouble cutting the cake, and had managed only to destroy it. I reached over to help her, because I felt sorry for her, but also because I wanted to busy myself with something else and hide away. Something about Uncle Daniel's eyes almost made me cry. They were dead, in some strange way.

Kajsa pulled the cake and the knife towards her as soon as I had served Signe. I didn't have the chance to serve myself.

"Have you talked to Thomas?"

"Ah, Thomas!" Uncle Daniel rolled his eyes almost like Wilma does.

"Thomas doesn't understand such things," he said, pushing a spoonful of ice cream into his mouth. "But I'm pretty sure he could do with the money. He hasn't written a word for the last five years, has he?"

The bang when Wilma thumped her hand on the table was so loud that I flinched.

Uncle Daniel too; he almost choked on his ice cream.

"Thomas is the only one here who's bothered about Henrietta!" Wilma shouted, standing up so quickly that her chair fell over. "You're only bothered about the money!"

Uncle Daniel didn't say anything, but Kajsa's face grew all white and stiff.

"Wilma, that's enough," she said quietly. "Go up

to your room. And you can forget about going to that party tonight!"

Wilma looked as if she had been slapped. Her mouth opened and closed a couple of times, but then it remained shut.

She stomped out and I heard the stairs creaking under her heavy weight as she ran up them. The ice-cream cake had been left in front of Erland and he had started eating it straight from the serving plate with his own spoon. I realized there would be nothing left for me, so I stood up and made for the door.

Behind me Uncle Daniel and Kajsa had started whispering again.

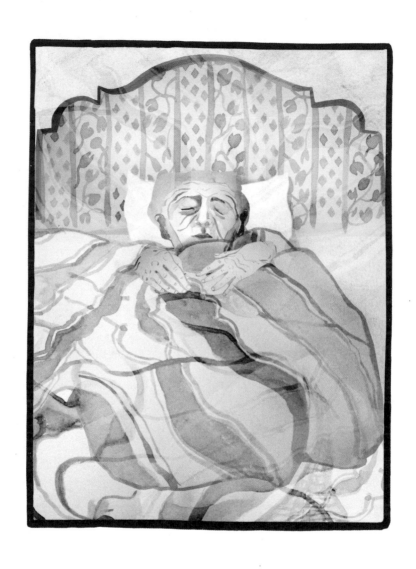

Her chest hardly moved.

Chapter Nine

IN THE CONSERVATORY

I left Wilma alone. At least for a short while. Even if she wasn't angry with me, I knew she would be sort of closed off and difficult to speak to. I went to see if I could help Dad instead.

He was sitting in Henrietta's room, of course, on his usual chair by the bed.

Henrietta was sleeping on her back, with her mouth half open and her thin hands folded over her stomach. She had been lying exactly like that the last twenty or thirty times I had seen her. Her chest hardly moved. Only the faint sighing of her breath showed that it was sleep, not death, that had closed her eyes.

"Is that you," Dad said.

He always said that, and it was not a question.

I pulled up the wheelchair that Henrietta no longer used and placed myself next to him.

"How is she?"

"All right, I think," Dad replied, like he always did. "Under the circumstances."

Sometimes I thought you could have made a film about all the times I'd come up to see Dad in Henrietta's room. You could edit the different days into one long sequence. In every cut our clothes would be different, and the light outside the window would change, but the words we spoke and Henrietta's immobile body would always stay the same. Like one never-ending, hopeless cycle.

But this time Dad did something different. He patted my knee and smiled a bit.

"How is Signe?" he said. "She seems more cheerful."

I nodded, but didn't say anything. I didn't know what to reply. It was probably the first time Dad had talked to me about Signe since he told me that she and Erland were coming over here with Uncle Daniel.

"She likes playing with you," he continued. "You can tell from the look on her face."

I looked up.

"What?" I said. "How can you tell?"

Dad waved his hand, as if he hoped that the gesture would explain what he meant.

"Well, she is happier now," he said. "More like a child. Less like... like Daniel."

I shrugged, but he was right. You couldn't ignore how Signe's ways of talking and moving had changed. But it was not because she had been playing with me.

"You know, Dad," I said. "About Signe..."

I said it slowly, because I didn't know how to continue. If I were to tell him about the dream and the wardrobe and the girl Hetty it would all sound completely mad. Or worse, woozy and childish, as if I was making it up.

"You just hope that Erland might start playing with you, too," Dad said. "He spends too much time by himself."

I realized that he hadn't heard me, and I didn't have the energy to start all over again.

"Erland doesn't like playing," I said and stood up. "He only likes destroying things."

Dad was still not listening.

"If only there were some toys, you could be in the garden," he said, raising his head. "Are you leaving?"

I nodded.

"I'm going to see Wilma for a bit," I said. "Good night."

"Night, night, sweetheart."

Only Henrietta's breath sighed behind me as I left the attic room.

"Wilma?"

I knocked harder. When I got no answer I opened the door carefully and saw that the room was empty. Perhaps she was with Kajsa?

The door to Kajsa's room was closed, but I could hear her inside whispering with Daniel. The last thing I wanted was to hear more of what they were talking about.

The whole time I was looking through the house for Wilma, Erland was somewhere nearby. You never saw him, but tiny, scratching noises revealed his whereabouts. Erland made me think of that summer when we rented rooms on a farm in Småland. It was hot and humid and there were so many flies you couldn't get away from them. At first you got angry and tried to whisk them away, but after a week or so you gave up and just let them creep around as they wished.

From the dining room I thought I could hear

Signe's laughter in the distance. She laughed the way you do when you're not alone. Like when you're sharing a secret with someone.

I knew I would find them in the conservatory even before I stepped through the glass doors. And there they were, sitting close together on the cast-iron bench, under a roof of wilting vines. Signe was dangling her legs, talking. Wilma sat beside her, listening.

"Ah, there you are."

Neither of them looked at me. It was as if I hadn't been there.

"But has she told you anything about herself?" Wilma said. "Who she is?"

Her eyes never left Signe, and I knew it wasn't me she was talking to.

"She's just a girl," Signe said. "She doesn't talk much."

"But her name is Hetty?"

Signe nodded. "That's what she said, anyway."

I felt like a thief sneaking up to them quietly and trying to sit down next to Wilma. It was as if I was trying to take something from them, and when I thought about it the feeling made me cross. Wilma hadn't even been there!

I leant a little closer to Wilma and felt her pull away.

"Don't meddle, Tommy," she said. "I'll give you hell if you snitch to Mum."

She didn't look at me when she said it, and something about her voice made me go all cold inside.

"I'm not a snitch!"

My voice had turned weepy and soft all at once, and that made me even angrier.

"Why should I snitch?" I said as I wiped my nose on the sleeve of my cardigan. "I don't care what you get up to!"

At this, Wilma turned to me. She put her arm around my shoulders and squeezed, a little too hard.

"Sorry, Tommy," she said in a softer voice. "But I need to try it too. Tonight, this very night."

I didn't even look at her. Above all I didn't ask her what she was talking about. I already knew. But at that moment, at least, it was completely true that I didn't care what she was up to.

"You will have to go on your own," Signe said, yawning. "I'm too tired tonight."

Her tired little voice made both Wilma and me check our watches. It was past nine, and Signe usually went to bed at eight.

"Come on, sweetie," Wilma said, taking her hand. "Let's go and brush your teeth."

"But this is real."

Chapter Ten

WILMA'S JOURNEY

I was sitting up in bed with one of Wilma's books on my lap to stop me from falling asleep.

No chance of that, though. First, I was still angry with Wilma, and second, I was worried.

Wilma had been nicer while we were putting Signe to bed, but something was weird about her. As if she was ill, or...

The same uneasy feeling that I had while we were brushing Signe's teeth returned: that the person I had always thought was Wilma was just a shell. Something she was about to grow out of; something alien and soon to be abandoned. I'm not often scared, but that feeling really frightened me.

In spite of sitting with the book open on my lap for hours, I doubt I read a single word. In any case I hadn't even turned a page when I heard the patter of Wilma's footsteps in the corridor just before two in the morning. In an instant I was out of bed and by the door.

Wilma stopped when she saw me in the doorway and her eyes gleamed in the light from my room. She was fully dressed and wearing her trainers.

"I won't get involved," I said, exactly as I had rehearsed. "I just want to make sure you'll be all right."

She put her finger to her lips.

"Shush, Thomas will hear you," she hissed, squinting nervously towards Dad's door. "Talk quietly."

I tightened the belt of my dressing gown and stepped across the threshold.

"Dad's upstairs with Henrietta," I said as loudly as before. "I'm coming in with you, just so you know."

Wilma stood still for a moment, and I could tell she was weighing different things up against each other. Plus and minus, for and against.

"Come on, then," she said at last.

Signe had obviously not explained it very well, because it was me who had to show Wilma the right wardrobe, me who had to turn the key and push her inside. And when we had been standing there inside with the mirrors for a moment and she tried to get out, it was me who stopped her.

"Not just yet," I whispered, grabbing hold of her. "Wait."

I wasn't really aware of what I was waiting for, but when the shift in the darkness came it was so obvious that I almost laughed out loud.

"That's it, we can step outside now," I said. "It's happened."

The reversed room was furnished almost the same as before, but the light from the window was brighter. There was a tone of sunshine in it, although it was still impossible to distinguish any colours on the carpets and the furniture.

Wilma stepped quietly in front of me, looking down at her feet, which left imprints on the soft carpet, looking around at the walls and the window.

"But this is real," she whispered. "Tommy, tell me it's real?"

I shrugged.

"I suppose it is in some way," I said. "It's just not the kind of reality we're used to."

The dressing table had moved, and there was another mirror on top of it replacing the gold-painted one that I'd carried away with me. The new mirror was larger and looked more modern somehow. The bottles and jars also looked newer, I noticed, with lids in pastel colours and labels in gold and red. Wilma sat down on the stool in front of the dressing table and tilted the new mirror until she could see herself in it.

"Like this, perhaps?" she whispered. "Perhaps I'm just supposed to sit here with my eyes closed?"

I leant forward and looked at the two of us in the dark glass. Wilma kept her eyes closed and her face turned slightly upwards, as if she were sunning herself. After a little while she started humming quietly.

"Mmm," she said. "That's nice. Brush harder."

I moved my gaze from our reflection in the mirror to Wilma's face with its eyes closed beside me. She looked the same, but somebody was standing in the shadows behind the stool, caressingly brushing Wilma's hair.

Hetty.

"You can read people too."

Chapter Eleven

IN THE LIBRARY

I wasn't at all frightened, actually.

Hetty smiled gently when she saw that I'd noticed her, and it felt quite natural to see her just standing there.

"Hello," I said.

Hetty blushed—at least it looked like it in the faint light—and met my gaze.

"Hello," she whispered. "Again."

I was happy that she remembered me, but also because of something else that I couldn't explain. Something about Hetty herself. She had the softest voice I'd ever heard, like silk against the string of a cello. It made you grow all warm inside, and I longed to hear her speak again.

But Hetty didn't say anything else while she was brushing Wilma's hair with long, steady strokes.

Wilma's eyes were closed the whole time and for a while I almost believed she had fallen asleep.

I stole a glance at Hetty and noticed that she had grown. The first time I saw her she had been as little as Signe, but now she was almost like me. Not quite, perhaps more like somewhere between Erland and me. She wasn't wearing the sailor dress any longer, but a blouse and a narrow skirt that stopped just below the knees. Her clothes and her hair, which was cut in a bob, made me think of old movies.

"Who are you?"

Without me noticing, Wilma had opened her eyes. She was looking straight at Hetty, but she didn't seem to be afraid.

"You know who I am," Hetty said. "You know me."

Wilma continued looking at her for a long time. Then she nodded.

"Yes, I do," she said. "But I don't really know how."

Hetty stopped brushing and took a bundle of velvet ribbon from her pocket. She held the ribbon carefully between her lips while she gathered Wilma's curls at the nape of her neck, and then she tied the ribbon around them in a bow. It looked really lovely, actually. I had never seen Wilma wear her hair like that before.

"Thank you," Wilma said and reached for a powder compact on the table. "You?"

Hetty looked up.

"Yes?"

"Can..."

Wilma hesitated and grew quiet. Then she handed the compact to Hetty and started again.

"Can you do something with me? I mean, make me prettier?"

Hetty took the small round compact and looked at it for an instant. Then she shook her head.

"Only you can do that," she said, putting the compact back on the table. "But I can show you how. Come with me."

At first Wilma hesitated. She looked quizzically at the bottles and jars on the table, and then at Hetty. But Hetty was already halfway out of the door, so Wilma got up and followed her.

I followed a few steps behind, through the corridor towards the hallway. The house was really just like Henrietta's. But the things that should have been to the left were to the right, and vice versa.

A house of mirrors.

"I've heard that you enjoy reading."

Hetty's question made Wilma look up at her.

"Read?" she said hesitantly and pushed her glasses onto the bridge of her nose. "Sometimes. Yeah, I suppose I do."

"But you do, Wilma," I said. "You read all the time."

Neither Wilma nor Hetty turned around. They hardly seemed to know that I was there.

"You can read people too," Hetty continued. "You hear all the things that they're not saying."

Wilma didn't reply, but she stopped and looked at Hetty.

"Not everyone can do that," Hetty said and held her arm. "It's a special gift."

She opened a door and entered. After a couple of moments Wilma followed, and then me.

We went into a room full of books, and I mean full from floor to ceiling. On all the walls apart from the one with the windows, there were built-in bookshelves with row after row of books, and other books were piled on the tables and in small, low shelves by the floor. It could have been messy, but it wasn't. There was an order to the wall of books' spines, which made the room calm and restful. I was certain that I had never been there before, but when I walked over to the wall with the windows I recognized where I was. The view looked towards the part of the garden where Dad had told me there used to be a rose garden when he was little. I realized that the room was the same as the one that was used as a dining room in Henrietta's house, only reversed.

"Sit down," Hetty said, pointing towards the sofa in the middle of the room. "Kick off your shoes and make yourself comfortable."

Wilma did as she was told, but it still didn't look all that comfortable.

"But there are only books in here..." she said. "You were supposed to show me how I could be prettier."

"Take a look at the books on the table for now," Hetty said as if she hadn't heard her. "I'll look for some good ones."

Wilma leant forward and looked suspiciously at the pile of books on the sofa table.

At first she just dragged her finger along the spines, and then she looked up. She wriggled out a thin green book with fabric covers from the pile and opened it.

I lay down on the sofa. It was lovely to stretch out next to Wilma, and nice to listen to her calm breathing right beside me. Apart from that the only sound was the faint scraping of Hetty every now and then moving the library steps she was standing on, or the rustling when Wilma turned a page. The feeling of sunlight was stronger in here, but I still could not see any blue sky outside the window.

How could it be day? It had been night when we entered the wardrobe.

It wasn't important. Night turned into morning, which turned into day in the house of mirrors too, but it didn't really matter.

In this room time could not alter anything. It was a comfortable thought, like Wilma's arm around my shoulders, and I fell asleep wrapped in it.

I slept. I don't know for how long, but when I woke up it was darker. Someone had covered me with a blanket, but Wilma had got up from the sofa. She was standing by the window with something in her hands. There was no sign of Hetty.

"Wilma?"

She turned her head.

"Come here, Tommy," she said, as if she'd been waiting for me to wake up. "Come and have a look."

My body was stiff and my feet stung and itched when I walked across the carpet. I stood behind Wilma and saw that it was a mirror she was holding. It was one of those oblong ones that you put up in hallways, with a simple wooden frame and barely a metre tall. We were both reflected in the mirror, along with the bookshelves behind us.

"Can you see?" she said.

I had to blink to stop my eyes from hazing over and all the time I wanted to yawn. I stifled the yawning and really tried to look.

"I see," I said. "It's you and me."

"Take another look."

I looked again, for a long time. And then I saw it.

Something had happened to Wilma. It was nothing peculiar, but she had changed. Her face was calmer, her neck straighter, her eyes clearer. To tell the truth, she looked just the same, but with one difference.

She was beautiful.

"How lovely," I said. "Did Hetty help you with the make-up?"

Wilma smiled. It was a smile I had never seen on

her face before, but it made me relaxed and full of hope.

"She helped me find my way home," she said. "This is me."

She waved her hand in front of herself and I couldn't tell if she meant her reflection in the mirror, or the room, or what. Probably everything.

"From now on this room will always give me a way to look at the world," she said. "Hetty told me so, and now I know that is how it is."

I didn't know what to say, so I nodded. It was true, I realized that. For my own part I hadn't changed at all, but the energy that streamed from Wilma was so tangible that it would be ridiculous to doubt it.

It struck me that the thing I'd been so afraid of had happened now, and that it wasn't so bad after all. Wilma had changed, but it didn't mean anything. If anything, she was more like my Wilma now.

She put the mirror down against the radiator under the window and reached out her hand for me.

"That's it, Tommy," she said when I took it. "We can go back now."

"I think they went into the conservatory."

Chapter Twelve

A Morning of Loss

Nobody woke me up, so I slept until half past nine, and when I finally woke it was to a low rumbling noise. It grew and disappeared, grew and disappeared in the corridor outside my bedroom, and I couldn't understand what it was.

In the end I kicked off the duvet, pulled on my dressing gown and opened the door.

Erland was standing at the end of the corridor, outside the half-open door to the dressing room. He was holding the handles of Henrietta's empty wheelchair and looking at me.

"What are you doing?" I said. "How did you manage to get the wheelchair down the stairs on your own? You know you are not allowed to use it."

Erland didn't reply. Instead he started running towards me with the wheelchair in front of him. It came faster and faster and the same rumbling sound that had woken me up grew stronger.

"Erland, cut it out!" I said, and stepped into the corridor. "Stop, and let go of the wheelchair!"

Something in his eyes alerted me. He wasn't going to stop. On the contrary, he hoped I would stay put so that he could run into me.

At the last moment I jumped back into my room. Erland didn't even slow down.

"You little shit!" I shouted after him.

At the end of the corridor he stopped and turned around.

"I hope you go to hell."

He said it so calmly, so completely without emotion, that I could think of nothing to say.

It wasn't a great start to the day, but it was going to get worse.

Dad was standing in the kitchen preparing lunch. For once he didn't seem to be cooking just for Henrietta, but for everybody. There were plenty of vegetables on the counter: potatoes, bunches of carrots, leeks and French beans. He must have gone to the market that morning, and that was probably when Erland had taken the wheelchair.

Uncle Daniel was sitting by the table reading the morning paper, so I didn't mention anything about what had happened in the corridor. It was no use talking about Erland when Uncle Daniel was around. He refused to listen and made sure Dad didn't listen to me either.

"Where is Wilma?" I asked when Dad smiled quickly at me over his shoulder. "Is she awake?"

Dad didn't reply at once, which gave Uncle Daniel the opportunity.

"Well, at least she was awake a little while ago," he said with one of his mirthless little laughs. "There was one hell of a racket here earlier."

I ignored him just the way he usually ignored me and kept my eyes on Dad.

"Where is Wilma, Dad?"

"I think they went into the conservatory," he said, with that anxious frown on his brow. "But perhaps you shouldn't..."

"Who?" I asked. "Wilma and Signe?"

Both Dad and Daniel looked surprised.

"Kajsa and Wilma," Dad said. "I think they probably want to be left alone."

I could hear their voices when I went into the

dining room. Somebody was angry, somebody was crying, but I couldn't make out who.

Wilma often quarrelled with her mother and I usually stayed out of it. It was always about such silly things. Like who had put a red sock in the white wash, who had watered an orchid to death, who won *Idols* four years ago, things like that. I never had the energy to take much notice.

But this time it sounded different. Not least because I heard my name being mentioned several times.

I grew more perplexed when I opened the door to the conservatory, because it wasn't Wilma who was crying. It was Kajsa.

"There she is," Wilma said as I entered. "Now you can ask her yourself."

Kajsa looked at me, but she didn't look as if she wanted to ask me anything at all. She looked as if she wanted me to get lost.

"Don't drag Thomasine into this, Wilma," she snivelled, wiping her face on the sleeve of her jumper. "I still haven't had an apology from you."

Wilma shook her head.

"I meant everything I said."

Her hair was still tied back with the ribbon that Hetty had wound around it and I still thought she looked beautiful. It was really hard to explain, because nothing in Wilma's appearance had really changed. But when I saw them both together, she was more beautiful than Kajsa.

"Wilma, you've got to speak to somebody," Kajsa said. "We may have to take you to hospital."

Wilma smiled. Her eyebrows rose and she looked surprised.

"To hospital?" she said in a voice that was completely calm. "Mum, do you think this is about me being ill?"

"Yes, I do!" Kajsa said, unexpectedly loud. "You come here babbling about mirrors and the truth and about your dad being dead and—"

"I didn't say that Kjell was dead," Wilma interrupted calmly. "I said that he's not alive. That's not the same thing."

"Whatever!" Kajsa shouted. "You don't talk like that about your father!"

"But it's true."

Kajsa lost it and started yelling so that you could hardly understand what she was saying. I have never seen her so angry. Nor could I tell what it was all about, apart from the fact that Wilma had obviously said things about her and Kjell.

Whatever it was, it could hardly have been worse than what Kajsa said to Wilma.

I didn't think a mother was capable of saying such things to her own child. I had only ever heard such things said in films. Throughout it all Wilma stood there without saying a word to defend herself. I got the sense that she felt sorry for Kajsa.

After a while Kajsa started crying again and walked out. She was still crying when the doors slammed behind her.

When Kasja was gone Wilma sank down on the bench where she and Signe had been sitting just the night before.

I walked over and cautiously sat down next to her.

"Wilma? What happened?" She sat with her gaze fixed on the lily pond in the middle of the conservatory. It held neither water nor lilies, and was just grey cement, but I knew it wasn't the cement that Wilma was looking at.

"Sometimes you have to tell it just the way it is."

I waited for her to continue, but she didn't.

"What did you tell her, then?" I asked, although I wasn't sure I wanted to know. "Why did Kajsa get so mad?"

Wilma turned her head. It was as if she only right then realized I was there.

"What did I tell her?" she asked. "The truth, of course. The whole truth."

"Did you tell her..." I had to stop and swallow several times before I could carry on. I didn't know why my mouth was so dry. "Did you tell her about the house of mirrors? About Hetty?"

Wilma looked at me.

"They'd never understand," she said. "They don't want to know. It's easier for them to think that I've gone crazy."

In a way it was a relief when she said it, because up until then I had not known who had been right. But something about the new-found confidence of Wilma's voice still worried me.

"Things will soon settle back down," I said, moving a little closer. "Come dinner time, Kajsa will have forgotten all about it."

Wilma did not offer any resistance when I took her hand, but neither did she squeeze mine back.

"But I won't," she said. "Things will never be the same again."

She sounded sad as she said this, but still determined. I felt apprehension rise within me.

Would Wilma leave now?

"Can't you tell her you're sorry, then?" I said. "That you didn't mean what you said? You only have to say it, it won't hurt you."

"Yes," Wilma said quietly. "Yes, Thomasine, it would."

She patted my hand and got to her feet.

"It will have to work, one way or another," she said, smiling a little. "They can't throw me out, can they?"

And then she was gone. I immediately realized that she would leave the house and go home, perhaps that very day.

I remained seated on the bench, feeling Wilma's absence like a dead weight in my stomach. It pulled me down, and I couldn't even turn my head when I heard the dry bamboo stalks rustling behind me.

Erland, of course.

It was probably half an hour before I could even stand up. I couldn't think, could find no words of comfort or explanation. Everything felt like a total loss.

But while I was sitting on that bench I realized something, even if I didn't know what to do with it: though it was true that my feeling of loss was related to Wilma having changed, it was not the cause. The feeling of loss was something to do with my being exactly the same as I was the day before.

The loss felt like a bubble around me.

Chapter Thirteen

WHERE IS ERLAND?

It was just as I thought, and an hour later Wilma's room was empty. Her books and clothes had been hastily packed in two large paper bags and only the mattress remained, stripped bare and abandoned on the bed. Kajsa's room had been vacated too, and the only proof of a former occupant was a faint smell of something sweet.

We were supposed to have Dad's vegetable bake for lunch, but when it was time to eat no one was hungry. Dad had escaped up to Henrietta. Wilma was nowhere to be seen, and Kajsa had already called for a cab. On my way through the corridor I heard her voice from the kitchen.

"It's this bloody house," Kajsa said in a whisper. "It's as if it's contagious. You saw what happened to Signe, didn't you?"

"Signe is fine."

It was Uncle Daniel.

"Perhaps," Kajsa said. "But what Wilma said was completely, utterly mad!"

I held my breath and heard Uncle Daniel sigh.

"But Kajsa, dear," he said. "You don't pay any attention to the kids, do you? Something good is worth waiting for, don't you think?"

"It's hardly worth it. I don't want to stay here!"

Kajsa's voice sounded harsh and you could tell that she was barely keeping it all together.

"You imagine things," Uncle Daniel said. "But just let me know if you want to give up your role. Such things can be arranged."

"Like hell," Kajsa hissed. "I will be back. But alone."

A little later I heard a cab's horn at the gate and went down the hall with Signe to say goodbye. Kajsa had only packed her own stuff and she looked the other way when Wilma came downstairs with her paper bags. But at least she was allowed to share the taxi. Only Signe and I waved.

We had the vegetable bake for dinner instead,

and it felt as if the kitchen had grown, or the lamplight was brighter. No pizza, no Wilma. Just Dad, me, Signe and Uncle Daniel, silent around the table. Erland didn't want any.

After dinner I managed to get Henrietta's ancient TV on the first floor going so that Signe could watch children's TV. Wilma had previously tried to watch TV a couple of times, but she had thought the picture quality was poor. It was a bit grainy and the colours were strange, but Signe didn't seem to mind. She curled up on the sofa, leaning up against me. I don't know if she had ever watched children's TV before. Uncle Daniel doesn't like TV.

It was nice being with Signe, but once I had put her to bed things felt twice as empty. I thought about going back to the TV, or even calling somebody from my old class, but I ended up sitting by the window on the landing with one of Wilma's books for the whole evening. Dad walked past every now and again, wondering if everything was all right, and Uncle Daniel asked a couple of times if I had seen Erland.

I answered them both that I didn't know.

The loss felt like a bubble around me and I could neither understand what I was reading nor what anyone said to me. It was not until after supper, when I was in bed trying to go to sleep, that something managed to burst through.

"Thomasine?"

The knock on the door was just like Dad's, but it wasn't his voice. I sat up in bed, pulling the duvet up to my chin.

"Yes?"

The handle was turned down and Uncle Daniel's face appeared in the gap.

"Are you sure you don't know where Erland is?" he said. "I haven't seen him all evening."

He didn't sound worried, just surprised, but a ripple went through my stomach like cold water.

"Neither have I," I said. "I really don't know."

Uncle Daniel nodded without looking at me.

"Goodnight, then."

When he had closed the door I lay back again, but I was fully awake. It was true that I hadn't seen Erland for several hours, perhaps not since lunch.

Most likely he was just hiding somewhere as usual, but what if he had hurt himself? What if he was trapped somewhere?

What if he was lying under water?

I closed my eyes and wandered through every room in Henrietta's house in my mind. There was nothing dangerous in any of them, really. Nor in the garden.

You could maybe get stuck in the mangle in the basement, but for that you would almost need to be two people. There was an old clothes chest in one of the bedrooms where somebody Signe's age could get stuck, perhaps suffocate after a while... But no, not Erland. It would be easy for him to lift the lid.

So where was he, then?

It was not until I had been lying silently in the dark for a quite a while that I noticed the noise. I realized that I had heard it several times without understanding what it could be.

Now I noticed that it came from somewhere far away, and it sounded like when you cry with your mouth closed. It was just a cry without a word or tone. I wasn't even sure if it was a cry for help, but I was sure about one thing: the voice belonged to Erland.

*The glass in each of the mirrors was not the still,
polished surface it had been before.*

Chapter Fourteen

THE MIRROR NEVER LIES

The wardrobe was as dark as ever, but something had happened. The glass in each of the mirrors was not the still, polished surface it had been before. Now shadows were billowing there, like blood swirling through water or thunderclouds being chased across the sky by a storm.

Erland was in the house of mirrors, I was sure of it. I could hear him screaming.

The transformation took longer this time, and the shift in the light did not offer any relief, as it had done before. On the contrary.

When I stepped out of the wardrobe I almost crashed into Hetty. She was standing just outside the door, dripping wet and shivering.

"He came through," she said weakly. "I don't know where he is."

The same wordless cry sounded from somewhere in the house again. Now I could hear both fear and pain in it. Erland sounded like an animal.

"We'll find him," I said, trying to steady my voice. "Do you have any dry clothes that you can change into?"

She nodded. "In my room."

For the first time I got to see Hetty's room, which was a mirror image of the same room on the second floor that I had chosen for myself. The bed was the same, and even a couple of the paintings above the chest of drawers. Apart from the reversal, the main difference was that Hetty's room felt a lot more like a home than mine.

I helped Hetty out of her soaking-wet clothes while she stood on the carpet, shaking from the cold. The water poured from her, as if she had been fished out of the sea moments before.

"What happened?" I said. "Where did all the water come from?"

She looked at me quickly, her eyes frightened.

"I don't know," she whispered. "I think it's him who does it."

Hetty was taller than me now, and looked almost

Wilma's age. When she wriggled out of the singlet with stiff, jerky movements I saw that she had grown tiny breasts.

I rubbed her dry with a cotton throw that I found on the bed and helped her into underwear and bodice, wool stockings with garters, blouse and skirt. I had never seen such clothes before, but Hetty pulled them on with practised movements.

When she had pulled on a knitted cardigan and buttoned it up to her chin she stopped shivering.

"How did he find the way here?" she asked. "Did you show him?"

I shook my head. "Erland eavesdrops," I said. "He sneaks around people and snoops out their secrets."

Hetty stood up, straightened the cardigan, and inhaled deeply. Then she closed her eyes for a moment, as if she was composing herself.

"Erland is a good boy," she said, reaching her hand out to me. "It's not his fault that it's inside him that darkness gathers."

I had never thought about Erland in that way, but it was true. He was an empty space where a darkness of varying depth mingled with blackness.

Hand in hand we walked along the darkened corridor, in the direction of the screams. They were coming more often now. I tried to switch on the light in the hallway, but nothing happened.

"He doesn't like the light," Hetty said. "He has made sure it's dark."

The moonlight shining through the stained-glass window was enough for us to see where to place our feet. And for me to see the traces left behind by Erland. A large pot lay smashed on the first landing, the flowers trampled into the carpet as if somebody had been jumping on them. On the walls were darker streaks from dirty hands and a picture frame hung askew and gaping above a sofa.

All of that was stuff that Erland could have done in the real world as well, even if he always tried to blame somebody else. But when Hetty opened the door to the basement, I grew scared. Scratch marks around the handle looked as if some predator had made them: deep grooves that shone white against the brown wood.

"I think he tried to get out," Hetty said quietly. "I didn't dare to open."

The light on the cellar stairs didn't work either, of course, but Hetty held my hand and led me downstairs. With each step Erland's screams grew stronger and more frequent. He knew that somebody was coming.

I had been in Henrietta's basement many times, but there were many things in the basement of the house of mirrors that I didn't recognize. The great mangle was still in the laundry room, but instead of a washing machine and tumble dryer there was a walled-in washbasin and a sort of press with a long handle. The larder was lined with shelves, and everywhere there were jars of jam and preserved fruits, sacks of flour, peas and dried beans. A wooden box in the corner smelled tartly of last autumn's apples.

Half the boiler room was full of coal to feed the fire; large chunks glistening in black behind a plank on the floor. The boiler itself was different too, old and sooty with a flap, flames swaying orange behind its grill. The firelight spread over the walls until they seemed to surge in the light.

"He's in there," Hetty whispered in my ear. "There, in the corner."

She pointed into the darkness next to the boiler, and I saw, but couldn't believe my eyes. How could the black, spider-like shape that had crawled into the corner be Erland?

Not until he cried did I realize it was true.

Perhaps it was his scream that made the flames of the boiler flare up. I don't know, but in any case it grew brighter. When the yellow light fell on Erland's face, I realized why he sounded the way he did.

Erland no longer had a mouth.

The lower part of his face was just smooth skin, which stretched and strained when yet another scream pressed up through his throat. His eyes were like they were before, but large with fear.

I couldn't help it. I started crying.

"What are we to do?" I whispered.

Hetty shook her head while she started pulling me slowly back towards the door.

"We can't do anything," she said. "Someone who loves him must come."

I stopped, but Hetty's hand held its grip on my arm.

"Uncle Daniel won't listen to me," I said. "He'll never come here with me."

Hetty pulled and I started moving again.

"I'll tell you what you should say to him," she said. "This time he will listen."

The taxi slowly started to move.

Chapter Fifteen

A Farewell

Henrietta's house was still, as if it were holding its breath between its high walls.

I was still not quite sure if I was fully awake, but my naked feet slapped hard against the floorboards in the corridor. Even here in the real world everything felt like a nightmare.

It was not until I entered the room that Erland shared with Signe and saw his empty bed that I realized that everything was true. Erland was no longer here on the outside.

Signe was sitting up in bed. Her hands were fidgeting with something invisible on the duvet and she seemed worried, almost like when she first came to the house.

"Signe," I panted, "I have to talk to Uncle Daniel!"
She looked up and her eyes were frightened.

"Dad's not here," she said softly. "He's looking for Erland."

"Where?" I said, trying to catch my breath. "Where is he looking?"

I could read the answer in Signe's eyes even before she whispered the words.

"In the basement."

It was easier to run downstairs. I took the steps in huge cat leaps, held onto the railing at the corners and rushed down the corridor towards the kitchen as fast as I could. I didn't really know whether my rushing would help Erland, but that was not why I was running.

I ran because standing still was too awful.

The cellar door stood open and in this world the lights were working. I lit every single one that I could reach and all the time I was crying Daniel's name.

He was standing in front of me as I turned a corner and I hardly had time to stop.

"Have you found him?"

Uncle Daniel was not his usual self. His arms, which usually hung limply down his sides, stuck out and jerked tensely, while his shoulders were pulled right up. He was holding a torch in his hand, and it blinded me.

"Could you move the torch, please?"

He lowered it impatiently. "But have you found Erland?"

I didn't know how to respond. My hesitation made him angry, I could see that, but I couldn't simply say yes or no. I had to tell him using exactly the words that Hetty had used.

"Thomasine, I'll have no more of this—"

"No! You must listen to me!"

The words came out in a shout, although I hadn't meant to scream. It worked.

"Erland is not here," I said quietly. "I will take you to him, but first you have to listen."

Uncle Daniel watched me with a look that swung between anger and some other quality, but he kept quiet.

"Follow me," I said, turning. "I will explain along the way."

On our way back up through the house I repeated what Hetty had told me, almost word for word. That our lives are shards in which only a piece of something larger is reflected. That there are parts of every human being that are hidden to themselves. And that we need each other to have the courage to see.

I had understood everything when Hetty spoke to me, but I felt in my body that Uncle Daniel didn't understand me now. And who could blame him? The things I said sounded insane; it sounded as if I were lying.

On the very last step before the second floor, I stopped. The strength that had borne me running through the house was all used up, and I couldn't believe in anything any more. Least of all what I had just said. When I turned to Uncle Daniel I saw that his eyes were frightened. They were almost as frightened as Signe's.

At once I could see what he was seeing. His child had disappeared and here was a girl he hardly knew— that he didn't even like—who babbled about mirrors and shards and invisible realities...

I closed my eyes and Uncle Daniel's grief and loneliness merged with my own.

"Is he alive?"

His voice was just thin air. Like the wind blowing through grass, but it made me open my eyes.

I nodded, although I wasn't quite sure it was true. If that thing I had seen with Hetty in the boiler room was Erland...

"I can't explain," I said. "You have to come inside with me."

"Come where with you?"

I didn't waste any more time on words. I had talked enough.

"Just come," I said, taking Uncle Daniel's hand.

I had never thought about the wardrobe being narrow, not even when I went in there with Wilma. But now I was totally aware of Uncle Daniel's big body pressing against mine, his heavy breathing, the heat that radiated from his pot belly and through my nightie into my back.

"Thomasine, I don't know—" he breathed, but I interrupted his faltering whisper with my own.

"Quiet! Can't you just stand still and be quiet, please!"

My eyes closed, I hoped, hoped, hoped that the transformation would happen this time as well. What would I say if it didn't? Or if I thought it had happened and it hadn't, and opened the door only to find that we were still in the same house where we had begun?

What if I had imagined it all? Perhaps I was really mad.

But when I opened the wardrobe door and stepped out onto the floor my foot landed in something cold and wet: a puddle of water that Hetty had left behind.

"Come," I said again, but this time I didn't take his hand.

Uncle Daniel followed me through the dark house of mirrors and I saw out of the corner of my eye that he was trying to understand where he was. A couple of times—by the smashed flowerpot on the stairs and when we passed an upturned sofa in one of the drawing rooms—I heard him trying to say something. I put my finger over my lips and indicated that he should walk on.

At the cellar door he stopped in his tracks, although I had already taken several steps down.

"Listen now, Thomasine, that's enough," he said, rather loudly. "What is this? Where are we?"

I shook my head.

"I don't know any more than you do," I said.

I continued down the cellar stairs, and when I had reached halfway I heard that Uncle Daniel was following. It ought to have made me relieved, but it only made me more anxious.

What would Uncle Daniel say when he saw Erland? And could anyone, least of all his dad, save Erland now?

"Who is she?"

Uncle Daniel's whisper came close to my ear.

"Who?"

"The girl! What is she doing here?"

It hadn't occurred to me that I ought to have explained who Hetty was or why she was standing there in the passage before us. I was just so happy to see her.

"Her name is Hetty," I said, and I pushed him past me. "She wants to talk to you, so listen."

And Uncle Daniel did actually listen while Hetty talked to him softly and gravely.

I had no idea what she said to him, but after a while I saw him nodding.

"I will try to talk to him," he said. "Erland is not an unreasonable child if you explain things to him in the right way. Where is he?"

Hetty's eyes were sad when she took hold of Uncle Daniel's hands.

"Is he your child?"

Uncle Daniel looked as if he didn't understand.

"I told you he is," he answered. "Why do you think I'm here?"

"Is he your child?" Hetty's voice was just as quiet when she asked the question a second time, but something anxious crept into it and I saw her hands squeezing Uncle Daniel's.

"What do you mean?" he said, pulling his hands free. "Are you sure we are talking about the same child? Short hair, blue eyes, rather—"

"Is he your child?"

Uncle Daniel fell silent and looked at her. I didn't understand how he could meet Hetty's gaze. I wasn't able to.

It was as if all the grief in the world was contained in those pale blue eyes; as if years of lonely weeping had gathered there.

"Is he your child, Daniel?"

I had time to breathe ten times before Uncle Daniel moved. He nodded once, bent his head and started crying with his face hidden in his hands.

"Then go to him," Hetty said. "Bring him home."

And Uncle Daniel went by himself into the dark room where Erland was.

132

I don't know what he saw in that boiler room. Perhaps he just saw Erland's usual self, or else he saw the same creature that I had seen. In any case, he stayed in the dark and after a while he started whispering.

Hetty sat down with her back against the wall with the boiler-room door and I lay down with my head in her lap. I was so dreadfully tired, but I couldn't sleep. It felt like hours went by as I lay there listening to Uncle Daniel's whispering voice. Sometimes he cried so much I couldn't hear what he was saying. Sometimes I heard, but not everything.

She didn't want me, Uncle Daniel whispered. *She left me when I needed her the most, and it hurt so much. I wasn't brave enough to let myself need you and Signe, even though you stayed with me. I was scared that you'd disappear and that it would hurt again, Erland. I'm sorry.*

The strange thing was that I understood everything Uncle Daniel said, even when the words were incomprehensible.

I understood in the way you understand music, and after a while the whispers rocked me to sleep, in the way the waves wash a bark boat towards the shore.

·

I woke in my own bed, and it was early morning. A humming sound could be heard in the street. When I walked up to the window and peeked through the curtain, I saw the cab waiting outside the gate with the engine running.

"Would you like to say goodbye?" Dad was standing in the doorway, fully dressed as if he had been up all night.

I didn't need to ask who was leaving.

Barefoot and in my dressing gown, I followed Dad down the stairs into the hallway by the main entrance. Sitting on top of a suitcase so large that she could dangle her legs was Signe. She looked up when I arrived.

"We are going home, Thomasine," she said. "The train is leaving soon."

"I know," I said. "What... Where is Erland?"

"There he is." Signe pointed behind me.

I turned around, and at first I couldn't understand what I was seeing. Uncle Daniel was walking through the drawing room with his arm around a boy I had never seen before. He was small and thin, and dressed in a coat and a knitted hat. The face was pale and his eyes were fixed on the floor in front of his feet as if he were afraid of stumbling.

Not until he was right beside me did I get it.

The boy was Erland, but he was not like before. All the dark that had lived inside him was gone.

Uncle Daniel had changed too. He was wearing his usual clothes, but it was as if he didn't fill them any longer. The coat hung from his shoulders and the trousers flapped around his legs when he walked. His steps were as cautious as Erland's, only slightly longer.

"Well, then," he said, glancing at his watch. "The taxi is waiting."

All the chill and spitefulness had gone from his voice, and it reminded me of somebody else's voice. It took me a couple of seconds to realize it was Dad's.

"We'll help you with the bags," Dad said. "Put on a pair of shoes, Thomasine."

Holding Signe by the hand and carrying her little cardboard suitcase in my other hand, I walked down the garden path towards the gate. Signe's hand was soft against my fingers and I felt how she was holding on to them.

"Are you afraid?" I whispered. "Would you like to stay with me?"

She shook her head without looking up.

"Erland is fine now," she said. "Dad and I will look after him."

I looked at Erland's face when Uncle Daniel carefully stretched the seat belt across his chest in the back seat. Signe was right. He was just a boy now.

When we had loaded all the bags into the boot of the taxi and I had helped Signe with her car seat and her belt, Uncle Daniel turned to me.

"Will you be seeing Hetty again?" he asked, so quietly that only I could hear.

I nodded.

"I think so."

"Thank her from me," Uncle Daniel said. "Tell her that I'm grateful for what she did."

I nodded again. Dad and Uncle Daniel shook hands and Signe gave me a hug before I closed the door behind her. I walked round the car and stood on the pavement next to Dad.

The driver put the car into gear and the taxi slowly started to move. The grit in the gutter crunched under the tyres and the car windows mirrored the pale blue dawn sky above us. Through the back-seat window I glimpsed Erland's pale face as the car glided past. His eyes were large and dark, and as they looked straight into mine his mouth formed one single, silent word.

Sorry.

I raised my hand in farewell, and they were gone.

The silence was me.

Chapter Sixteen

THE SILENCE

The days after everyone had left felt unreal. The empty rooms in Henrietta's house were in constant shadow, in spite of the late summer sun outside the windows. A strange silence rolled through the halls and corridors, and even the smells were gone.

Not until the third evening did I understand. I was sitting alone in Wilma's empty room, where the bedding was still folded neatly on top of the mattress, when I realized that it was not the silence that was alien, but everything else that had been and gone: the sounds and voices that had occupied the house while the cousins were there had been the exception. The silence was familiar, like an old cardigan.

The silence was me.

I know that I cried a little there on Wilma's bed, but I actually can't remember at what point I decided to go back to the wardrobe with the mirrors. I can't even be sure that I actually made any decision at all. Suddenly I was just sitting there in the house of mirrors, on the sofa under the stained-glass window on the first-floor landing.

Hetty was sitting next to me and on the table in front of her were half a dozen paper boxes full of photographs. A couple of empty photo albums were opened up and she had placed a glue bottle with a brush lid on a napkin.

She was almost an adult now. A young woman, wearing beautiful clothes. The blouse was made of cream silk, and the skirt of a soft, grey woollen fabric. She had kicked her light-coloured pumps onto the carpet and she sat with her legs curled under her on the sofa. She was so beautiful that I almost started weeping again.

"Have you been crying, Thomasine?"

I shook my head, but realized that of course she didn't believe me. My eyelashes were still straggly and I was sniffling all the time. I hadn't been aware that Hetty knew my name.

She didn't ask anything else and for a while we sat quietly as she picked up bundles of photographs, flicked through them and put them down again.

"Well, what are we going to do about all these?"
she sighed. "I have been thinking for a long time
that I should sort them out, but I don't know where
to begin."

I picked up the bundle she had just put back into
the box. They were old photographs, black-and-white
with a funny serrated edge. Most of them seemed to
have been taken outside, in a garden or some kind
of park, and in one of them a young man in white
trousers was doing a handstand on a chair. He had
braces over his shirt and his trouser-legs had slipped
down to reveal a pair of tartan socks. I didn't know
who he was; I didn't recognize him even when I
turned the photo upside down and saw his face the
right way up.

"Why not start from the beginning?" I said. "Is
this the oldest box?"

Hetty shook her head.

"There are many that are older," she said, pulling
one of the boxes towards her. "The year and month
are written on the back of each one."

"Well, then," I said. "Why don't we just sort them
from the oldest to the newest?"

Hetty's face lit up when she looked at me. She

wasn't smiling, but there was joy in her eyes, which made her look as if she was.

"You're so clever, Thomasine," she said. "What would we do without you?"

I shrugged my shoulders.

"Ah," I said. "It's just what you do, isn't it?"

In silence, we sorted through the photos of these strangers.

Neither of us said anything, and the sounds we made when we grabbed another bundle and sorted through them were so faint that you could hardly even hear them.

The oldest pictures were from the end of the nineteenth century. They were mounted on thick cardboard, and all of them had the names of photographic studios on the bottom. In that box there were no exteriors or photos of actual rooms. Single men and women, children in groups, and large families had gone to the photographer to get their pictures taken. They had old-fashioned clothes and hairstyles, and sometimes somebody wore a uniform or a student's cap. A young man in a suit, with a centre parting as straight as a nail, rested a glowing white straw hat on his lap. Everybody looked thoughtful, almost dreamy. I once asked my dad if people were more serious back then, but he answered that it was probably more to do with the fact that you had to sit still for so long in front of the camera.

There were only a few dozen cardboard photos from each decade to start with, but then, as we got into the twentieth century, something must have happened. Suddenly there were bundles of twenty or thirty pictures a year, and the photographs were thinner and smaller. They no longer showed just people, but streets, houses, beaches and boats. Some were photos of pets, especially a little black dog, and those pictures were blurry, as if they had been taken by children.

"Look, they are off to Denmark in this one," Hetty said as she showed me the photo. "They had taken the night train to Elsinore."

It was a photo of two men and three women standing in front of a white railing on a ship, with the sea in the background. They all wore hats, and the men were dressed in suits and ties. A little boy in shorts and a sailor shirt was sitting on the deck in front of them, and on the back of the photo it said *June 1922*.

"Who are they?" I asked, handing it back. "Do you know their names?"

Hetty looked surprised, but that invisible smile remained brightly on her face.

"Of course I know their names," she said. "I'll write them down when we stick them in the album."

A little later, she started gluing the photos into the album, writing a few lines under each photo. *Benjamin and Gottfrid on their way to scout camp in Furusund*, it might say. Or *Margot and Asta with Spot under the pergola*. She seemed to know the name of every single one of them.

I carried on sorting through them for a while, but then I got fed up and opened up the album that Hetty had just finished. To begin with I flicked through it mechanically, but after a little while something made me stop. I went back to the beginning and studied each photo carefully, and then I realized that the same faces appeared again and again. They were reproduced on page after page, but with variations. The younger people in particular changed so much within a few years that I had to go back and check their names to know that they were really the same people. They were in the country stroking cows, they went to the funfair, they graduated from school and university, they got married and did their military service, had children, moved, travelled. Lived.

As if falling in a dream, I realized that what I was flicking through was the lives of human beings. Only tiny slivers of each one, of course, but still real lives.

As real as my own.

Hetty had put the cap back on the glue bottle and was sitting watching me. She saw that I had understood, and this time she really smiled. At that moment the sun shone through the stained glass of the hallway window and the rays fell across the room like tiny twirls of colour and light.

Life is always there around us. So many human lives that they are impossible to count, and yet we can always perceive the unfathomable space in each one of them.

"I know," Hetty whispered, although I hadn't said anything. "I know, Thomasine."

Her whisper pushed me across an invisible boundary, and suddenly I collapsed. I collapsed into the soft pillows, and cried.

It wasn't the usual type of weeping, the kind that only goes on for a short while and makes little difference. This was like a spring flood, a hot wash with many rinses, the draining of a water tank until it was empty. I cried so that my whole body shook, I yelled and sobbed, and all the time I was thinking: Now. This is when it happens. Everything is changing now, this is when I become new.

I think it took quite a while. Afterwards I felt clean, but when I sat up and looked around I realized that the room hadn't changed at all.

Hetty was sitting where she had been sitting before; I was in just the same place, too.

"That felt good, didn't it?" Hetty whispered as she offered me a hankie. "You needed that."

I wiped snot and tears from my cheeks until they were dry.

"It only helps for a while, though," I said. "And I can't go on crying forever, can I? I thought something would happen."

Hetty looked at me curiously.

"Like what?"

"I don't know," I said, patting my eyes dry with the hankie. "That I would change like Wilma. And Signe and Erland."

Hetty got up and slipped her feet into her pumps.

They fitted her so well that she only had to wriggle her foot to get them on.

"That all depends," she said as she glanced at her watch. "Wilma and Signe and Erland all had things inside them that they needed to discover."

"And what about me?" I said. "Have I... haven't I got things inside me that I need to discover?"

It felt really horrible to know that. Was there really nothing worth discovering inside me? Was what you saw all you got?

"I'm sure you have," Hetty said. "But you are not the problem here."

I looked at her. I really didn't get it.

"What do you mean, I'm not the problem?" I said. "Why not?"

Hetty was already on her way down the stairs. Just before turning the corner, she halted and looked back, one hand resting on the banister.

"It's not you who's standing in the way of your life, as it was for your cousins," she said. "It's someone else."

And then she was gone.

I recognized every single picture.

Chapter Seventeen

HENRIETTA'S VOICE

I must have wandered several miles through Henrietta's house that day. For the first time I really paid attention to the rooms; I saw that somebody had figured out how everything went together. The hallway and the hall led to the dining room that led to the parlour and onwards up the stairs to bedrooms and bathrooms. Everything was in perfect order for following a person's movements through the day, through the night and into the next day.

For the first time I saw that Henrietta's house had been built with one single purpose: that people should live in it.

And Dad and me, what were we doing here? Were we alive? Dad didn't come down from Henrietta's room until late in the evening, and by then he was so tired he could hardly speak. We ate a bit of whatever was in the freezer, mainly cocktail sausages and frozen vegetables that I had fried up before. But at least it wasn't pizza.

"Thanks, sweetheart," Dad said when he had finished. "Leave the dishes and I'll do them when I come downstairs."

"Are you going back up to Henrietta again?" I said, glancing at the clock, which had just turned ten. "Shouldn't you try to get some sleep?"

He rubbed his eyes with his fingertips.

"I can't," he said. "She won't last long now."

He had never talked like that before. I realized it must be serious.

It was probably just a matter of hours.

"Go to bed," I said, standing up. "I'll sit with her. I'll wake you if anything changes."

Dad looked at me with red-rimmed, blank eyes.

"But you need your sleep," he said. "You are a growing girl."

I turned on the tap and put the dishes in the sink.

"I'm not sleepy," I said. "It feels as if I've been sleeping for far too long."

.

Henrietta was lying in the same position as the last few times I'd seen her. On her back, her hands clasped over her stomach, her mouth half open and her eyes closed. You couldn't tell whether she was dreaming. Her face looked calm, so at least she wasn't having nightmares.

I knew Dad turned her over sometimes so that she wouldn't get bedsores, but most of the time she lay as if she were already resting in her coffin. She looked comfortable, and suddenly I realized how envious I felt of her.

The thought made me sit up straight.

Was it true? Did I really envy somebody who was about to die? In perhaps just a few hours?

Yes, I did.

I wished my face could have been as free of longing as Henrietta's, that my hands lay as still as hers. At least then I wouldn't be wishing for a lot of things that would never happen.

I finished the albums, Thomasine. Would you like to see?

It was Hetty's voice, and it came from somewhere in the room. Or else it only existed in my head. But I didn't care either way.

151

"Yes," I said aloud. "Where are they?"

There was no answer. My gaze wandered from Henrietta's white bed to a stool by the bedside table. A pile of old leather-bound books were lying there—they looked familiar. Were they what Hetty meant?

I picked up the top album and opened it carefully. No, it must be wrong. The pages were yellow and smelt old, and Hetty's albums had been as good as new. Without thinking, I turned to the first page.

The face in the picture almost made me jump. That centre parting, as straight as a nail.

The straw hat, white like cream cake, rested on the young man's knee. I had seen the same photo before.

It was me who'd pasted it there.

I only had to turn a few pages to be sure. The worn album I was looking through now was the same one I'd helped Hetty fill with pictures. But just a few days ago the covers and pages had been brand new.

It was the same with the other albums in the pile. I recognized every single picture and hardly needed to read Hetty's wriggly handwriting below each photo to know who the people were. In a group shot of children on a lawn from around the time of the First World War, I noticed a chubby girl with plaits. She might have been five years old, and she wore a white dress and apron. Henrietta, it said.

I turned my gaze from the album to the old woman in the bed. There was no similarity at all between Henrietta in the photo, taken on a summer's day in another world, and Henrietta beside me. Had that wrinkled face on the pillow really been hiding under that rosy child's cheeks that the camera caught almost a hundred years ago? Well, yes, I think it probably had. All our future faces are hiding behind the one we see in the mirror each morning. Even this evening a change will occur, so tiny we can't see it.

But the camera does.

With renewed interest I flicked through the albums looking for the stages of Henrietta's transformation, and found them at varying intervals. Henrietta as a schoolgirl, dressed up as a witch for Easter, as a girl scout with a sooty nose, in a rowing boat surrounded by white water lilies. In the next album she was suddenly dressed in grown-up clothes, she was bicycling, laughing with girlfriends who were probably long dead. Then came the photos from drama school, the plays, the films. The photos of Henrietta increased in number each year, some private, others taken by film studios and magazines. The rest of the family was there too, growing old and having children, but it was as if they were lurking in the shadows while Henrietta was standing in the light.

When I reached the Sixties, shortly before Dad and Uncle Daniel were born, the photographs of Henrietta stopped abruptly. The last photo showed her sitting at a café table in a piazza in some warm country. Italy, perhaps. She smiled into the camera one last time, untouchable and blindingly beautiful.

Then she disappeared from the pages of the album.

Instead of photos of Henrietta there were photos of children. Tiny, round, smiling kids caught in fading colour photographs. To my surprise, I recognized some of them from Dad's album at home. There were baby photos of him, Uncle Daniel and Kajsa, holiday photos and school photos, sometimes a postcard with a child's handwriting and arrows pointing to a specific hotel window. They must have sent them to Henrietta, and she must have collected them. She, who had never had any children of her own, had preserved the photographs of the youngest members of the family as carefully as if they had been her own.

There was Dad, smiling over the handlebars of a moped. His fringe was hanging down over his eyes and he had long points on his shirt collar. In the photo below, Kajsa was sitting in the sun on some steps. She was wearing flares and a white T-shirt with a smiley face on it, and she looked about Wilma's age. Even Uncle Daniel looked young standing on a jetty somewhere, proudly holding a perch impaled on a stick.

I flicked through the pages faster. I had never seen these photos before. There were quite a few of Dad, as a boy, a teenager, a young man. Mum appeared in a holiday photo at the end of the Eighties, and right at the end of the last album was a photo of a laughing, dark-haired girl who'd lost her front teeth.

It was me.

I could even remember when Dad took the picture. At the funfair, the summer before Martin was born.

With fumbling, frightened fingers I turned the very last page of the last album.

And there it was.

The photo, the only one that existed of all of us together. Mum and Dad younger and close together, me with Martin on my lap. Our smiling faces so open that it hurt me on the inside.

At that moment, in that fraction of a second when the photo was taken, we'd believed that we'd always be happy.

"Thomasine."

The whisper ought to have frightened me, because it was real. It came from within the room that I was sitting in, but I wasn't afraid. I did not even flinch when Henrietta's scrawny hand left its nest on her chest and shakily settled on my arm.

"I'm here," I said as I leant closer towards her. "Would you like me to get Dad?"

Henrietta's head moved a few millimetres in either direction, indicating a no.

"It is..." she breathed, and I had to put my head right by her mouth in order to hear her. "It is you I want to talk to."

I sat up.

"Me?"

My surprise was real. Even when Dad and I

had first visited, while Henrietta was still up and about, she had seldom talked to me. Not that she was unkind—on the contrary—but she was already entering her own world.

Sometimes I hadn't even been sure if she knew who I was.

"You have to bring him in here," Henrietta whispered. "Now, tonight."

Was she awake, or was she talking in her sleep? I studied her closed eyelids, as if they could give me a sign.

"Show Thomas the mirrors," she breathed, every word a sigh. "Take him to the conservatory and ask him this..."

The last words were so faint that I would never have heard them if I hadn't put my ear right beside her mouth. But I heard, and nodded that I had understood.

Henrietta's eyes opened for a second, and when her gaze met mine I drew a deep breath. The world shook beneath us when I realized.

Henrietta was Hetty. Hetty was Henrietta.

It just happened.

Chapter Eighteen

THE LAST JOURNEY THROUGH THE MIRROR

At first he was just lying there, face down across the bed, fully dressed, his arm trapped underneath him. His body rested like a dead thing on the mattress, and I tried not to think about death while I pulled at his hand.

"Dad," I said, shaking him hard. "You've got to wake up!"

I swallowed the fear that burned in my throat. Dad wasn't dead, just sleeping, and if I continued pulling he would wake up.

"Please, Dad, wake up!"

And then suddenly he turned over on his side, lifted his head and was fully awake.

"Is it Henrietta?" he said, in his normal voice. "Is she?..."

"She's sleeping," I said. "But you have to come with me."

I had planned it like that, just to get him out of bed and drag him through the corridor to the octagonal room before he had time to think. I didn't want any questions.

It worked. We were already inside the wardrobe when Dad had woken up enough to start asking questions.

"But why are we here?" he mumbled. "Thomasine, what are we—"

"Shush," I whispered. "Don't talk!"

Dad coughed, the way he always does when he gets unsure.

"What do you mean?" he said carefully. "Am I not even allowed to ask what—"

"No, you are not."

The shift in the light had come and gone and I pushed open the door impatiently with my bum.

"You can come out now, Dad," I whispered. "Come on, get out!"

He followed me out of the door, and I was uncertain whether the transformation had actually occurred this time. The room looked almost the same as the one we had left behind: empty of furniture and with muck along the walls. It was not until I noticed that the windows were on the wrong wall that I knew we were really in Hetty's house, not Henrietta's.

Something told me that we would not meet Hetty this time. Even if I had suspected it as I entered the wardrobe, I was still disappointed. There were so many things I had wanted to ask her. About myself and about her; about the people in the photo albums. How did they became strangers to each other?

But this was not the right time for that kind of thing. I was going to bring Dad to the conservatory, and the only question I was going to ask was the one Henrietta had whispered in my ear.

As we walked through the house I felt Dad hesitating, but I couldn't let him stop. Not until we entered the glass doors of the conservatory. It was impossible to drag him any further.

"Thomasine, what have you done?"

Dad was standing dead still on the cement tiles next to the lily pond, looking around. He pulled away his hand and crossed his arms over his chest as if he was cold.

"What do you mean, 'done', Dad?"

Dad pointed at the lush vine above us and at the pond, which was full of water.

"I haven't done anything, Dad," I said. "It just happened."

He lowered his hand and looked around, but he didn't say anything.

"Dad," I said, trying to collect myself. "I'm going to ask you a question and you have to give me the honest answer."

He just stood there looking at the plants winding around the cast-iron pillars above the still surface of the pond.

Then he blinked.

"If I can," he said.

We stood in silence, facing each other in the moonlight. I felt like you do just before you jump off a very high diving board; perhaps Dad did too.

Then I took a deep breath and let it out.

"Dad," I said. "What do you wish for most of all?"

Dad's gaze slid away, and even before he opened his mouth I knew he was going to lie.

"Well, you know," he said evasively. "An end to all wars. That everyone could enjoy good health, things like that."

I didn't say a thing. I just stood there and let his words fall to the ground without even trying to catch them. He could tell, of course, and I saw him slump. Now he knew that he wasn't going to get away so easily.

"What do you mean, then?" he said at last. "Wishing for things? Money? Well, I don't."

"I know that," I said. "But what do you wish for most of all?"

Dad looked at me and suddenly something glinted in his eyes. It was only there for a moment, but I felt my back prickling with anxiety and expectation. I hadn't seen that determined, almost stern gaze in Dad's eyes for years.

Not since Martin died.

"Forget it, Thomasine," he said, turning around. "I don't want to play this stupid game."

He went and sat down on a bench, the same one Wilma and Signe had been sitting on, and I let him sit by himself for a while. Then I went over and sat down cautiously next to him.

"I don't think it's a game," I said.

Dad sighed and threw up his hands. "But it's completely pointless," he said. "Why should we go around making wishes?"

"Why not?"

"Because they'll never come true!"

There it was again. The spark that went out long ago lit up in Dad's eyes for several seconds before it died out again.

"Life's not like that, Thomasine," he said. "I know that you don't understand, and perhaps the point is that you shouldn't. Yet."

He grew silent and looked down at his worn-out slippers for a long time before going on.

"But life's not like that," he repeated, more quietly this time. "It turns out the way it does, and all you can do is try and do your best."

I was silent too for a while. Not because I didn't know what to say, but because sometimes you need to leave silence between the words.

"You can still make a wish," I said. "Perhaps it doesn't even matter if it comes true. Perhaps it's the wish itself that is important."

Dad was looking at me now, and his gaze was full of doubt. I knew it meant that he was thinking about what I had said, and I knew that was good.

"What do you wish for most of all, Dad?" I said so quietly that it was almost a whisper. "Most of all?"

164

He slumped again, shaking his head.

"No, I can't say."

"Yes, please say it!"

My voice was still no more than a whisper, but now it sounded eager and childlike. I could hear it myself.

Dad shook his head again without looking at me.

"It's no use," he said. "I can't."

Suddenly a tear fell from the tip of his nose and without a sound landed on the cement between his slippers.

Dad was crying.

I couldn't remember the last time he had cried without hiding it from me.

"Dad, you can do it. Say it."

He cried harder now, really weeping. There was no noise, but his whole body was shaking. As carefully as I could, I placed a hand on his arm.

"Say it, Dad."

"I wish—"

He didn't get any further before his voice broke, but he tried again.

"I would really like to hold him again. Just for a little while."

The words were no more than a whisper, but I understood.

"Martin?" I said. "Do you mean Martin?"

Dad nodded, but by now he was crying so hard he could no longer speak.

I don't know how I happened to look at the pond, I just did.

And there he was.

Martin, my little brother, was lying just below the surface. He was wearing his red waterproof trousers and a knitted jumper. I remembered the jumper, and I remembered the feeling of Martin's small round hands.

But although he was lying under water, nothing was like it must have been that awful day when Dad found him in the pool. This was not an ending.

Martin was lying there smiling at me, just as I remembered him.

"Dad," I said, nudging his arm cautiously. "Look, Dad."

Dad lifted his head and looked towards the pond. At first he was completely still; he stopped crying in the middle of a sob, stopped breathing. Then he flew up from the bench and before I could stop him he had stepped into the pond.

166

"Martin!" Dad shouted. "No, Martin! No!"

He crouched down, fumbled for the child's body under the water and lifted it out. All the time he screamed, and the screams cut like thorny poles right through me.

Dad must have screamed just like that on the day that no one had heard him. But this Martin was not floppy and lifeless in Dad's arms. He wriggled and his hands held onto Dad's cardigan. Then he laughed.

Martin's laughter. The sound was like an echo from another life, something that another Thomasine had heard. But I recognized it.

Oh, how I recognized it!

"Martin," Dad said, clutching him tightly. "My God, how you scared me, Martin."

I stood behind Dad's back and saw how Martin threw his arms around Dad's neck. He smiled with his tiny rice-grain teeth, like he always did when he played a trick on us, and hugged Dad hard, hard.

"Thank God," Dad whispered. "Thank God."

Martin pressed his face against Dad's neck, and Dad's hand stroked his back outside the wet jumper. I remembered when Mum knitted that jumper and how impatient I'd been for Martin to grow into it.

They were exactly his colours; the same blue as his eyes and the same sun-bleached wheat yellow as his hair.

Suddenly I saw the stripes in the jumper turn blank and merge into one. Martin's downy neck lost its colour, his hands around Dad's neck turned transparent like water. For a moment Dad held a body of water in his arms; a perfect, transparent sculpture of Martin.

Then the surface broke and the water fell to the floor in a shower of glittering drops, and when they fell against the cement tiles they sounded like rain. A still, warm spring rain, washing the world clean.

Dad just stood there with his eyes closed, his clothes soaked, his arms bent as if he were still embracing a child. I watched his closed eyelids, frightened of what I might see in his eyes when they opened. Would he be the same as he had been just after Martin's death? Back to those weeks when he couldn't get out of bed?

Neither of us spoke. Dad kept his eyes closed and I kept watching. And then he opened his eyes, and in that instant I knew that it was all over.

The grief that had been in his gaze for so long was still there, but I saw something new as well. Or rather, I saw something that had been missing for so long that I almost had forgotten what it looked like.

Life. There was life in Dad's eyes again.

So slowly and still, so completely without pain.

Chapter Nineteen

A Kind of an Ending

*H*enrietta died at dawn, between night and day. A window was open in her room, and the air that sifted in was cool. The first blackbird of the new day started singing in the garden, and I thought I saw a smile on her sleeping face as she heard it.

Dad and I held Henrietta's old hands in ours and watched life seeping out of her for almost an hour. There was nothing fearsome in it. On the contrary: it went so slowly and still, so completely without pain. Her breathing became weaker and weaker, until it stopped altogether.

Dad pulled the sheet carefully over her face, and then we went downstairs together to get something to eat. The first ray of sunlight broke through the mosaic in the stained-glass window on the stairs just as I passed it. I stopped and let it shine on my closed eyes for a couple of seconds.

Henrietta had lived a long life, and now she was gone. The earth kept turning, leaving behind an empty space in the world. What else can you say about the life of a human being?

I lean back and look at the words I have written. It feels like a kind of ending, but it's too early to know. Perhaps I'll recall something that I'll want to add in due course.

I'm writing this sitting in my special study. It's dark around me, but the screen on Dad's old laptop—which is mine now—lights up my face. I know that it's just a computer screen, but I can't help thinking of it as a window, or perhaps a door. A shining opening into all the days I have not yet lived.

It has been almost two years since the morning when Henrietta died, and I'm fourteen now. Older than Wilma was then, and we are still living here. In the end it turned out that no one apart from Kajsa wanted to sell Henrietta's house, so we divided it into flats instead. Mum, Dad and I live on the second floor, and Daniel, Signe and Erland live on the floor below. The ground floor is divided into a shared sitting room and a flat, which Kajsa sold. A young Iranian family lives there now, with a little girl who Mum says looks exactly like me when I was that age.

Mum turned up at Henrietta's house after only a couple of days, and she and Dad took care of all the practical matters. There was a lot to be done, of course. Mum said that there usually is when somebody dies. A lot of everyday things that no one has thought of suddenly turn up and have to be dealt with. In the evenings I lay under the table in the dining room and listened to their calm voices. They made phone calls, found solutions. After a while Dad started writing again, and then he bought a new computer. In the afternoons I'd write my diary on his old computer, while I listened to him tapping on his keyboard in the next room. It was so like everything I've ever dreamt of that sometimes I couldn't be sure it was for real.

Daniel came back too, with Erland and Signe. Signe was pleased to see me, and Erland was just an ordinary little boy. He read a lot, and that's something I had never seen him do before. Daniel had got some new clothes and glasses and for the first time I heard him speak of Erland and Signe's mum. She lives in Germany with a new man, and Erland and Signe visit her in the school holidays.

I didn't see Wilma again until a year after Henrietta died. I didn't even speak to her on the phone, and I thought that perhaps she was angry with me. At first I tried to understand why, and then I tried to be angry as well.

But then one summer morning when I came out into the garden, Wilma was sitting on the steps talking to Mum and Dad. I shouted out and threw myself around her neck. I couldn't stop myself.

We talked all day, and Wilma told me that she wasn't angry at all. At least not with me. But she had quarrelled a lot with Kajsa and her dad. They wanted her to study economics at college and go into sales like they had, but Wilma refused. When the time came to choose a new school, she picked an art college, which was a long way away, and now she lives in a completely different town.

Wilma comes and stays quite often during her holidays, and I think she sees us more often than her own parents. She says that she loves Kajsa and Kjell, but that she has to be allowed to decide for herself. She says that she always felt like that, and she probably believes it is true.

I have tried to talk to Wilma about everything that happened with Hetty in the house of mirrors, but it is as if she has forgotten. Everyone else seems to have forgotten, too. But I remember.

I look through Henrietta's albums sometimes, and sometimes I still play hide-and-seek with Signe and Erland. It's just an ordinary game now, and the wardrobe with the mirrors has been furnished with wallpaper, a rug, a chair and a table.

It's like a real little room.

My study, actually.

The mirrors from the wardrobe hang in various rooms around the house, and when I stop in front of one of them I can sometimes see that I look older. My eyes are as dark as ever, but I can see a hint of Hetty's gentle gaze underneath. They look into me saying: wait a while, it will get better.

It's good to think about, but I don't have any great desire to grow up, like Wilma does. Life is what it is, and there is no specific day when it starts, is there?

Well, yes. Sometimes there is, actually.

The day we all long for most of all, Dad, Mum and me, is the eighteenth of August. Or at least some time around then, towards the end of the summer. That's when the baby who's growing in my mum's stomach will be born, and I will be a big sister again.

As soon as the baby is old enough I'm going to take it out into the conservatory and we can sit on the bench and see how nicely Dad has fixed the pond, with new tiles, a new water-treatment system and plenty of water lilies. We will sit there, the baby and I, and I will tell the baby about our brother Martin, who disappeared.

I will show the baby the photo albums and talk about all the people who have lived in Henrietta's house before us. I will point at their faces and speak their names, just as Hetty wrote them down.

And who knows, if the baby wants me to, I may make up stories about all the people who will live here after us. There won't be any magnificent adventures about princesses and wars and magic, just stories about being born and living and dying. Adventures get no greater than that, I think.

MÅRTEN SANDÉN was born in Stockholm in 1962 and spent most of his childhood in the university town of Lund, in southern Sweden. He has been writing, in one way or another, more or less full-time since his early twenties.

Starting out as a professional songwriter for music publishers in Europe and the US, Sandén began writing children's books in the mid-1990s. *The Petrini Detectives*, a series of mysteries for Middle Readers, was launched in 1999. Since then, he has written around thirty more children's books, ranging from picture books to novels for Young Adults. His work has been translated into Danish, German, Russian and English.

Mårten Sandén is a member of The Swedish Academy of Children's Book Writers and The Swedish Crime Writers' Academy.

He lives in Stockholm with his wife and daughter.

MOA SCHULMAN has one foot in the world of images and another in text; she studied Literature and Linguistics at Stockholm University, and illustration and graphic design at Konstfack. She designs for print, illustrates for children, and publishes books in her own Dockhaven imprint.

PUSHKIN CHILDREN'S BOOKS

Just as we all are, children are fascinated by stories. From
the earliest age, we love to hear about monsters and heroes,
romance and death, disaster and rescue, from every place
and time.

In 2013, we created Pushkin Children's Books to share these
tales from different languages and cultures with younger
readers, and to open the door to the wide, colourful worlds
these stories offer.

From picture books and adventure stories to fairy tales
and classics, and from fifty-year-old bestsellers to current
huge successes abroad, the books on the Pushkin Children's
list reflect the very best stories from around the world,
for our most discerning readers of all: children.